DARK MAGE

AVALON

WEB OF MAGIC

Book 11

DARK MAGE

RACHEL ROBERTS

Seven Seas

DARK MAGE

Published by Seven Seas Entertainment.

ISBN: 978-1-934876-75-6

Cover and interior illustrations by Allison Strom

Interior book design by
Pauline Neuwirth, Neuwirth & Associates, Inc.

10 9 8 7 6 5 4 3 2 1

Printed in Canada

1

"*Vogue!*" Kara Davies struck a dramatic pose. With a bright twinkle, the waistline of the red halter sundress tightened into a perfect fit. Even though the dress set off her long, golden tresses and bronze tan, it still didn't feel right. A mountain of dresses, skirts, and shirts were piled on the floor of the mirrored dressing room at Fashion Fallout.

Her friends, Heather, Molly, and Tiffany, stepped out of the other three stalls and peered into hers. They were shopping for the major event of the year, the end of school dance taking place at the Ravenswood Preserve. Kara's idea, of course.

"Kara, that's like the thousandth dress you've tried on," Heather complained.

"Very unlike you," Tiffany noted.

"So true." Kara bit her lip. The girl in the mirror was not usually indecisive. Blond and radiant, Kara was normally confident, competent, and always cool. She had connections—her dad was Stonehill's mayor—academic chops, *and* full-on popular cred, the queen bee of her school. Kara was also a worker-bee. After school, she managed the Ravenswood Animal Preserve. Summer tours for the animal sanctuary were booked for weeks in advance and the town of Stonehill was getting good buzz about its "haunted" tourist attraction. To top it off, Ravenswood was only a few weeks from getting full landmark status.

So why was Kara stressing out instead of bubbling with joy?

She had thought some shopping time with her BFFs would make her feel better. But no matter what she did, she couldn't shake the feeling that something was coming. And it probably had big teeth.

"I can't decide on a dress till you decide!" Tiffany whined, looking over several outfits she had picked out.

"Ditto," Molly agreed with a shake of her short dark hair.

"I know." Kara eyed her reflection in the floor-length mirrors. This time, she saw beyond the perfect-teenager facade. The girl who stared back at her had a secret hidden deep inside. This Kara was a mage, a girl who possessed *real* magic.

Heather, Molly, and Tiffany had never met this Kara, nor did they have any idea that the Ravenswood Preserve sheltered magical creatures from another world. That was a secret shared only by Kara and two other teens, Emily Fletcher and Adriane Charday. They, too, had been chosen as mages, protectors of magic and the magical animals—a huge responsibility that weighed heavily on Kara's mind.

She glanced back at the mirror and realized what was wrong with the dress—the halter-top concealed her pendant—a pink, white, and red unicorn jewel sparkling on a silver necklace. She always wore the gem. It had powers and symbolized her connection to magic and her place in that world. She was the blazing star, the centerpiece of an ancient prophecy that had set her on an incredible quest. She'd taken an oath to complete it, a promise bound by more than words.

She flashed on Lyra, a sixty-five-pound, winged magical cat—with the freshest smelling, most perfectly groomed coat of dazzling orange and lustrous black spots. She couldn't imagine her life without her closest friend, or the scores of other magical animals who loved the mages and depended upon them. Emily was the healer of the trio, Adriane the warrior. As the blazing star, Kara had to admit, she was the most powerful. She'd been the first to reach Level Two, bonding with her paladin, Starfire, an elemental fire stallion. She couldn't fight like Adriane or fix things like Emily, but the magic loved her, believed in her, and needed her. Never in her life had she felt so truly a part of something so real and important. And after all, that was her destiny, wasn't it?

The mages had been chosen to find the source of all magic, a place of legend and myth called Avalon.

As Kara, Adriane, and Emily had learned, many realms existed along a network called the magic web. Once upon a time, magic flowed from its center: Avalon. But now Avalon was gone, mysteriously missing, and magic no longer flowed where it was needed. Unless the mages could find Avalon, the web would completely unravel and fade away—taking whatever magic was left.

Whoever found Avalon would control a new, stronger web and *all* the magic.

And the mages weren't the only ones looking.

From the strands that still remained, the evil Spider Witch was weaving her own web, pulling more magic under her control with every passing day.

The witch's former ally, the Dark Sorceress, was also up to something; Kara could feel it. She shared a connection with that monstrous half-human, half-animal woman.

That alone was enough to give her nightmares. But what really haunted Kara was that the quest to save the web might fail because of something she herself had done. The mages needed nine power crystals to enter the Gates of Avalon. They'd found five of them, but in a moment of anger Kara had destroyed one. Her magic had flared out of control leaving them one crystal shy.

Kara shuddered. The fate of every world on the magic web, even Earth itself, depended on the recovery of *nine* crystals, not eight. What if it was all her fault that the quest for Avalon failed?

Focus, she told herself. The important thing now was to find the four crystals that were still missing. They needed to work together, but the healer, the warrior, and the blazing star hadn't exactly been the Three Mageketeers lately.

During their last adventure, Kara had made a judgment call—she'd temporarily taken control of their friend Zach's magic, a decision that had surprised and angered Adriane. Kara had used her blazing star powers exactly as she was supposed to and saved hundreds of baby sea dragons. Instead of thanking her, her friends acted like she'd suddenly turned into Darth Vader. What the heck was she supposed to do? If she hadn't used her magic, it would have been her fault for not doing anything. She just couldn't win.

Why was it so hard for them to believe she wanted to do the right thing?

Kara knew better than anyone that she had made mistakes. She had betrayed the others more than once, and she, of all people, understood how powerful her magic truly was. The incident on Aldenmor bothered her more than she wanted to admit. It exposed her weakness—she didn't always know how much magic was enough, and when she was using too much.

Kara straightened her shoulders and walked from her stall to the floor-length mirror. All her life she'd juggled tons of different activities, from friends to school to cheerleading to interning at the mayor's office, and she'd always made it work. Somehow she would make all the magic stuff—including Emily and Adriane—work out too. Somehow, she would find the strength she needed. When the final battle for Avalon came, the blazing star would prove herself to her friends once and for all. Even if Emily and Adriane didn't understand the sacrifices she had to make. Even if they didn't understand how hard it was to keep secrets from her three oldest buds.

"What's the big secret, Kara?" Tiffany fluffed her blonde hair in the mirror.

"Huh?" Kara blinked, snapping out of her reverie.

"Who are you bringing to the dance?"

Kara's face flushed to match her dress. Her friends chuckled knowingly.

"I knew it!" Molly squealed.

Tiff grinned. "Whenever you think about a cute boy, you're a million miles away."

"Spill it, girl," Heather ordered. "Who is he?"

Kara smiled weakly. "You guys don't know him."

Disappointment spread across her friends' faces. She had always told them about her crushes—they'd spent entire nights talking about nothing else—but this time it was different. How could she explain that Lorren, the hottie she wanted to bring to the dance, had, uh … green skin? Or that he wasn't exactly human, but a goblin who lived in the Fairy Realms?

"I bet Emily and Adriane know him," Tiffany huffed.

Kara wished she could tell them the truth. She didn't know how many more secrets could she keep and still expect Heather, Molly, and Tiffany to be her friends.

"Look, there's something you should know—" she broke off as white-hot light flashed behind her eyes.

"I knew it, this is too sugar-plum fairy." Heather wrinkled her nose at the tank with sequin embroidery she was wearing.

"No …" Kara stammered.

The mirror flashed, spilling bright twinkles along the clothing-strewn floor. Pinpoints of light swirled around Kara's waist and into her unicorn pendant, making her heart pound. This definitely wasn't a call from Adriane or Emily, but it felt similar, as if someone were trying to connect with her unicorn jewel—or use it.

"Lyra!" she cried out in her mind.

"What is it?" the cat's silky voice answered instantly.

Kara shook her head, quickly scanning the dressing room. Everything looked normal. She and her friends were the only ones in there. *"Um …what are you doing?"*

"I'm helping Adriane and Dreamer in Owl Creek Meadow."

"Fine!" She couldn't call her friend here even if she really needed her. Flying leopards and malls did not mix.

7

"Whatever." Tiffany glared at Kara and smoothed her outfit. "I'm buying this."

"Did you get new batteries?" Molly stared as bright pink sparkled from the unicorn jewel.

Kara nodded, watching a second wave of lights dance across the mirror.

"I'm going to try on that other dress," Heather said.

"Good, go in there." Kara swung open the door to Heather's stall and—*Woosh!* The mirror against the back wall fell away, melting into a vast landscape of flickering stars. Kara's jewel glowed as she felt herself being pulled toward the brilliant lights.

"Ah!" Kara yelped and slammed the door shut.

Her friends looked at her.

"Wrong stall."

Kara herded the girls to the next stall, opening the door a crack to peek inside. Lights glimmered along the mirror's surface. Something had locked onto her jewel and was following her through the mirrors!

"Don't go in there!" Kara stopped short and slammed the door in Heather's face.

"But you just said—"

"Make up your mind!" Molly snapped.

"Um," Kara leaped inside the dressing room and locked the door. "I have to try on another outfit."

"You have so got to lay off the Frappucinos, K," Heather said.

Kara faced the mirror, bracing herself for whatever was

about to happen. But the lights had vanished. She peered closer. Her skin had taken on a distinct pale green glow.

"What's with this new foundation?" Kara wrinkled her nose.

"You look great," Kara's reflection answered.

"Thanks, I've been moisturizing." Kara preened, then froze.

The shiny surface rippled like water as someone suddenly tumbled from the mirror into the dressing room!

"Ahhhhh!" Kara screamed. She backed against the wall, then stopped, staring in shock as she realized who'd just come through the mirror: a pretty teenage goblin girl. Her green skin was flushed, her short dark hair was mussed and tangled. Beneath her velvet sorceress's robe, she wore jeans and a baby doll T-shirt that said "Tinkerbell."

"Hi, Prin—!"

Kara clamped her hand over the goblin girl's mouth.

"Kara, are you all right in there?" Molly called out.

"Fine! I mixed purple with red." Kara looked at her friend. "Tasha, what are you doing here?" she whispered.

The goblin sorceress was supposed to be on Aldenmor guarding the power crystals the mages had already found.

Tasha leaned forward holding a blinking handheld device. "I needed to get here fast, so I locked my crystal tracker onto your jewel. These mirrors are so primitive."

"Don't you see where we are?" Kara squeaked.

Tasha's black eyes scanned the small dressing room. "This isn't your bedroom?"

"Hey, Kara," Heather said. "We're moving on to shoes."

"Uh, I just realized I have to go to Ravenswood," she replied.

"We'll go too," Molly said eagerly.

"No!" the blazing star blurted.

Sensing her friends' shocked silence, Kara peeked out of the dressing room.

Heather, Molly, and Tiffany stood there, arms crossed.

"We thought this was our day together!" Tiff scowled. "You're always with Emily and Adriane."

"We're just sorting out stuff for the summer tours," Kara tried to sound casual. "I'll call you later. We'll go over the dance prep."

"Sure," Heather snapped, her green eyes filled with confusion and hurt. She linked arms with Molly and Tiffany. "We're getting used to shopping without you anyway."

Kara's heart sank as her buds stomped away. How was she going to make this up to them?

"Ooo, pretty!" Tasha spun in front of the mirror, holding a lavender dress in front of her sorceress's robe.

"Tasha, what's going on?" Kara asked.

The goblin stopped in mid-twirl. "I've got big news that will change everything!"

"What is it?"

Tasha held up her magic tracker, showing Kara a series of blinking lights. "I found the power crystals."

Kara's eyes opened wide. "How many?"

"All of them."

2

$\mathcal{E}$MILY FLETCHER DRUMMED her pencil on the dark wooden table, pretending to pay attention to Rae Windor, who droned on ... and on ... and on.

"I like science class and math and English too and next year I'm going to direct the high school musical. I hope it's *West Side Story* I love that show I'd die to play Maria or at least play lead tuba and—"

"That's nice," Emily replied absentmindedly, suddenly realizing the other girls in their study group had moved to a different table.

"Everyone's talking about the dance at Ravenswood," Rae prattled, "but who I am talking to—of course you know all about it."

Emily snapped to attention. Thank you, Kara, for

something else to work on. She was about to answer Rae, but the wiry-haired girl had already moved on.

"What's so important about gorillas?" Rae eyed the books Emily had chosen to research her science paper.

"Well, they're highly intelligent, social animals, and they're endangered."

"You know so much about animals." Rae gazed at her admiringly.

"My mom's a vet," Emily reminded her.

"You should get a special school award for working at the preserve," Rae declared.

Emily leaned back in her chair and eyed Rae warily. "I thought you didn't like Ravenswood."

Rae squirmed. "All the kids are working there now, I mean you know, Molly and Tiffany and Heather. Even Aunt Beasley doesn't think it's so bad anymore."

"That's a shock."

Beasley Windor was a haughty and outspoken member of the town council. For some reason, she was against the preserve's very existence.

"She said it's magical," Rae whispered conspiratorially.

"What?" Emily blurted.

"Shhh!" A couple of students shushed from across the library.

"You know, like special."

It was special all right. Emily ran her finger over the rainbow jewel on her silver bracelet, the only clue to the other life she led.

"You think I could work there too?" Rae asked shyly. "With all the cute animals like your ferret?"

"Sure, Rae." Emily gazed at the stacks of books splayed before her. All this research on civilization destroying natural habitats was starting to make her queasy.

Everyone knew about Ravenswood now. The tours had gone too well, booked solid through the summer. What would happen when she, Adriane, and Kara were no longer there to protect it? Would all the animals and the magic become extinct? Like the snow leopards or the giant pandas, or even elephants! They might all soon be gone—forever.

Two worlds on a collision course. The last of the great animals needed wild places to survive, but the world of humans continued to grow, consuming the natural resources of the planet. You didn't have to be a genius to determine the winner.

She kept hearing the voice of Marina, the water Fairimental, over and over in her head. *The web is almost gone. You are the last hope, the last mages.*

A familiar fear flared in the pit of her stomach as she thought about Aldenmor, its precious magic, the life-blood of so many creatures and animals, threatened by encroaching dark forces. Emily and her friends had been chosen to protect the magic so Aldenmor and other places along the magic web could survive. But for how long?

Kara was related to the fairy queen. It was no surprise that she had become the blazing star. Her magic was amazingly powerful, making everyone around her shine. Adriane had warrior DNA. The girl had no fear. Emily had never met anyone who had faced more heartache and risen above it to keep fighting on.

And herself, the healer, finally understanding her true magic. A month ago she'd had an adventure on the magical world of Aldenmor, becoming a Level Two mage and bonding with a wonderful unicorn paladin protector named Indigo. Indi was created from the Heart of Avalon, the only living power crystal. Emily had learned to actually see the colors and patterns of magic, something not even Kara and Adriane could do. The image of a bright blue and green pattern flashed in her mind, making Emily flush. It was the magical aura of her new friend, a very cute merboy named Marlin. He was busy training other merteens and their bonded sea dragons on Aldenmor, and he reported regularly to Emily on his progress.

Everything the mages had accomplished would be for nothing if the Spider Witch and the Dark Sorceress found Avalon first. Emily would have a key part to play in saving the magic web, something that excited and scared her in equal measure. It was up to her to heal the fading web, using her new talent for weaving magic. She had a chance to protect thousands of animals, to make sure the natural order was balanced and strong. It was a huge responsibility. What if she failed?

At least she'd know where to go after they found the

power crystals. The Heart of Avalon remained on a lost island, the Gates of Avalon, and would guide the mages there. And what *was* Avalon? No one they'd met so far, human or magical, good or evil, could tell them anything factual about the mysterious home of all magic, or what they were supposed to do when they got there.

It seemed like she was treading water, going nowhere. She felt like she might explode if something didn't happen soon.

"Whoa, that's cool!" Rae said excitedly, pointing to Emily's wrist.

The healer gasped. Her heart-shaped jewel was blazing with color!

Smiling nervously, she moved her hand under the table. "It reacts to light."

A quick glance showed that her jewel was back to its normal, subtle shine. She frowned. Another false alarm. Ever since she'd become a Level Two mage, the gem on her wrist had been acting strangely. She could be sitting in class, helping her mom at the veterinary office, or just eating breakfast, and this creepy feeling would wash over her, like someone was trying to connect with her. That's when her jewel would start to glow. Quick as lightning, the feeling would pass as suddenly as it had come.

She could have asked Kara and Adriane if their jewels had acted up after they'd reached Level Two, but lately things had been pretty tense between them. Kara and Adriane had kept their distance since their fight

on Aldenmor. And Emily had refused to be put in the middle of their arguing yet again.

She sighed, her mind going in circles around this all too familiar problem. Kara and Adriane were opposite sides of the same coin. Their magic wouldn't even work together without Emily there to buffer them. She only hoped they would put aside their differences and come through for each other and for Ravenswood in the end.

"I'm going to get a book." Emily got up and headed toward the back of the library. As she turned down a long aisle, the fluorescent ceiling light abruptly flared and dimmed, buzzing as it cast flickering shadows over the lacquered floor. She stepped back, peering nervously up and down the aisle.

"Is someone there?" she whispered.

But the aisle looked deserted.

She checked her jewel. It wasn't pulsing in warning.

Calm down, she ordered herself. If anything dangerous
was nearby, her gem would warn her. Wouldn't it?

Focusing on the books, she searched for the last title
on her list. And there it was, just out of reach on the
top shelf. She stood on tiptoe and grasped the heavy
volume.

"Gotcha!" She snagged the book from the shelf—and
froze. Two red eyes glowed at her from the other side of
the shelf.

Emily jumped back, the book tumbling from her
arms. The eyes disappeared; the creature they belonged
to was rushing down the aisle, coming straight at her!

In a panic, Emily stumbled, tripped over the book and
fell.

"Dark witch!" the monster cried.

Horrified, Emily stared at the beast towering above
her. Its bear-like body was covered in coarse black hair.

Red eyes glowed from a face with a long snout and sharp fangs. Around its thick neck hung a leather strap with yellow and blue feathers. But there was something worse than the way it looked: dark magic radiated from the creature. Emily could see it. She winced at the power swirling around it in a blood-red halo.

"Stay away!" Emily raised her jewel.

The creature halted a few steps from her, lowering its huge arms. "I have come to you."

Emily gulped, unsteadily rising to her feet. "What are you? How did you get here?"

"I heard your call, dark witch."

Emily backed against the bookshelf. This creature wasn't the first one to call her that. Ancient mermaids on Aldenmor had said the same thing.

"I don't understand. How did you get here?" she repeated.

"The portal leads to you."

"What portal?"

The creature turned its snout to the far wall. Behind the door marked "Faculty Only" a purple glow pulsed in dark waves. How could a portal have opened here? Only certain fairy creatures and unicorns could open portals at will.

"Emily, want to get some ice cream?" Rae rounded the corner and stopped in her tracks.

The monster snarled and spun around, claws extending as it charged the defenseless girl.

"No!" Emily shouted. Blue and red lightning streaked

from her jewel, locking onto both Rae and the creature. Girl and beast froze, unable to move or scream.

"Leave her alone," Emily ordered, slowly stepping between the creature and Rae. The beast's magic flashed through her rainbow jewel, clouding the bright colors.

But it obeyed her instantly, stepping back and retracting its claws.

Emily loosened her hold.

"It's a monster from Ravenswood!" Rae blubbered, tears springing from her eyes. "I don't want to be eaten."

"I am a descendant of the most fearsome race of warriors," the creature hissed. "I do not eat children."

Rae seemed to ease a bit.

"But in your case I would make an exception."

Rae sobbed.

"Quiet!" Emily flicked her wrist, sending blue magic glittering around Rae's head. Rae froze, mouth wide open in a silent cry.

This was exactly what Emily had feared! Two worlds had collided all right—in the middle of the Stonehill school library!

A gust of wind blew the faculty door open, revealing the magical gateway.

The creature shifted his red eyes to Emily. "You must come with me."

Emily's heart raced. She had to get this thing out of here! Her gem sparked as the portal suddenly began to shrink.

Moving her fingers, she released soft tendrils of magic. "What is the farthest place away from here that you can think of?"

The beast's gruesome face scrunched up in thought. "World's End…"

"Go there, now!" Emily ordered.

Blood-red eyes locked onto Emily, the creature's fierce will testing the strength of her spell. But Emily's magic was too strong.

"As you wish." The monster lunged through the glowing portal just as it swirled shut, vanishing with a blast of icy wind.

Rae stared at the empty space, dumbfounded.

What was she going to do? Emily fretted. There was no way she could explain herself out of this one. She ran a hand through her curly red hair, wishing desperately that Rae had never seen the creature. Her rainbow jewel flared in response.

Emily glanced at her jewel, then at her still-frozen friend.

Concentrating, Emily reached into Rae's thoughts. Random images flashed by— lunch in the cafeteria, soccer practice, band practice, coming to study in the library. Pushing the unimportant thoughts aside, she locked onto Rae's memory of the monster.

She had discovered this mind trick on Aldenmor, and although she felt uncomfortable using it, she had no choice.

"You didn't see anything weird," Emily said evenly, her jewel casting a greenish glow over Rae's face.

"Ravens—" Rae stopped in mid sentence, jaw slack, eyes glazed.

"You had a totally normal afternoon."

"—wood ... totally normal." The girl slumped against the bookshelf.

Emily felt the memory slipping from Rae's mind like smoke, until it disappeared completely. Hand shaking, she lowered her jewel.

Rae pushed away from the shelf in confusion. She blinked at Emily as if seeing her for the first time today. "What's up, Em?"

"I have to go." Emily turned and fled, snatching her backpack and racing outside into the warm spring afternoon.

Heart pounding, she took a few deep breaths, trying to calm down. She had needed to use her magic on Rae, hadn't she? It freaked her out, reaching into the girl's mind. But right now she had to deal with the fact that a monster had portal-popped right into the library. For all she knew, beasts could be popping up all over Stonehill. She ran to the bike rack, hopped on her ten-speed, and took off, her rainbow jewel glinting darkly in the sun.

3

S UN-WARMED GRASS CARESSED her paws as she stood in the open field. She sniffed the early summer breeze, relishing the crisp pine and wildflower scents of the Ravenswood Preserve.

"The portal field is full of flowers." Dreamer mischievously crammed his snout into a patch of tiger lilies the mages had planted this past March.

"I can see that." Adriane laughed as her vision became a blur of vivid orange.

Off in the brush, her keen ears picked out the rustle of scurrying animals and the faint whisper of the stream beyond. With a surge of energy, she was loping across the field. Trees and branches zoomed past as her low, sleek body raced through the forest. Sunlight blazed across the treetops, spilling along the branches as if every tree were glowing with vitality.

Adriane wanted to howl with pure joy. She had never felt so whole, so complete, so right. She felt she could run forever, a wild thing, connected with the forest that surrounded and protected her.

"Steady, warrior," Lyra's soft voice called in her mind.

In a whirl of light and shadow, Adriane's vision returned to where she stood, half a mile from Dreamer. She stomped her hiking boots on the forest floor, taking a moment to adjust to her own two-legged body.

The warrior rubbed her forehead, letting the dizziness wash away. She smoothed the glossy black hair hanging halfway down her back.

"You were slipping away." A large leopard spotted cat sat beside her, green eyes filled with concern.

"I ... it was so awesome, Lyra!"

"You and Dreamer are the only ones who can do this," Lyra said. *"But you have to be careful. I won't always be there to help you back."*

"Thanks." Adriane rubbed the cat's silky neck. "But it wouldn't be as much fun without you."

Caring for every inch of the preserve took a lot of time and energy, so Adriane had been practicing seeing through Dreamer's eyes to cover more ground and speed up her daily inspections. She had discovered the ability to actually merge with her packmate, something she hadn't been able to do as a Level One mage. It was beyond incredible, seeing the world through enhanced mistwolf senses, feeling so connected to the forest and the spirit that lived there. Adriane and Dreamer had been fine-tuning the process, the warrior eagerly pushing forward, seeing how far this new connection could take them.

She didn't believe it was dangerous, as Lyra seemed to think. Real danger was the landmark commission denying Ravenswood its seal of approval. Adriane had a personal stake in its being granted landmark status. This was her home.

The commission would soon send a representative to inspect the property. There were boundary marks to maintain, road repairs, debris cleaning, and checking trees for insect, disease or storm damage. Adriane was determined to show off the healthiest forest this side of Yellowstone National Park!

Once Ravenswood received landmark status, the forest could never be razed, and nothing could ever be built on it. But it was also her responsibility to protect the preserve from another kind of danger, one more destructive than any outside force—dark magic.

Adriane had learned that Ravenswood sat on a key point along a complex pattern of magic—the magic web. The preserve was the only place left where magic still flowed from the web to Earth. She lived here now with her grandmother and all the refugee animals that had come to Ravenswood for shelter.

The Spider Witch had tried to take over the preserve but the mages and their animal friends had stopped her. But the Dark Sorceress and the Spider Witch were gathering their forces. Securing the power crystals and finding Avalon came down to one thing for the warrior: keeping Ravenswood safe.

"When do we learn to fight, Packleader?"

Adriane whirled around—she'd been so lost in her thoughts, she hadn't realized she had company. A bright blue duck-like quiffle flapped its wings in excitement. A group of other magical animals gathered by her side. To them, she was the packleader.

"Being a warrior doesn't always mean being a fighter," Adriane told them. "A warrior must also be strong in mind and spirit."

"Packleader, how do we know the forest spirit is even here?" another quiffle queried.

"The spirit of Ravenswood is all around us." Adriane closed her eyes and opened her arms wide to embrace the magic. A gentle breeze tugged at her long hair. "If you listen you can hear her."

All the animals stopped and closed their eyes.

"I hear wind," Eddie, a blue bunny-like brimbee, whispered.

"Be the wind." The warrior swayed, gently dipping her arms as if she were floating.

The animals all swayed and dipped with her.

"I hear birds singing," Rommel the wommel said.

"Be the birds." Moving in a circle, Adriane waved her arms like wings. The animals trailed behind, arms and wings flapping.

"I hear the river!" Rasha, a quiffle, called out.

"Be the river." Adriane crept low, moving her arms in a swimming motion. The animals followed, with Lyra doing a perfect feline crawl.

"No baths without Kara," Lyra insisted.

Adriane laughed as the animals piled around her, hooting and giggling.

"You see, you can all touch the spirit of Ravenswood. The forest will tell you when and where there is any trouble."

"But what about using *real* magic, Packleader?"

"Right." Adriane stood and dusted herself off. "Protecting Ravenswood takes physical skills too." She surveyed the eager group. "And today, I'm going to show you how."

"Yes!"

"Ooo, magic lassos?"

"Death ray?"

"Fire breathing?"

Adriane smiled, pausing for effect. "We are going to grow flowers."

"What?" The animals squawked and honked, confused.

"Keeping the forest strong means knowing how to enhance its natural beauty," the warrior continued. "Besides," she unrolled a map marked with her list of repairs. "We need to fix the rest area by Mirror Lake. Let's move out!"

Heading down Hidden Falls Trail, she looked over her shoulder at the line of animals marching happily behind her. Three dozen quiffles followed by a herd of hopping blue brimbees, long-eared deer-like jeeran with purple and green stripes, five pegasi, several red koala-like wommels, and one confused peacock.

A smile spread across her face as she noticed delicate flowers in an unmistakably familiar shade of gold. Ever since Adriane's first bonded animal—a mistwolf with golden eyes named Stormbringer—had become the spirit of Ravenswood, the warrior had noticed subtle changes throughout the forest. The clearing where Adriane and Storm had first met was always lush with the most colorful flowers in the whole preserve. Branches filled with leaves never shaded the flat rock where Storm had loved to soak up the sun. Storm was also Adriane's paladin, a powerful protector forever connected to the warrior and her wolf stone.

Lyra padded up beside her, two small quiffles hitching a ride on her back. *"Her presence here is stronger than ever,"* Lyra purred, her emerald eyes scanning the vibrant forest.

Adriane's heart surged with happiness and she impulsively hugged the cat. "I love our home."

For the first time Adriane felt totally confident about who she was and what she was doing. And no matter where her adventures took her, Storm would be here to guide her home.

A snowy white owl glided overhead carrying a little stick figure—literally. It was made up of twigs and leaves.

"Hi Ariel." The warrior waved at the owl.

"Hooody," the owl answered.

"We have fourteen new birch trees and six new swans!" The twiggy figure spoke excitedly, reading a list projected from a turquoise crystal hung around his neck, his Handbook of Rules and Regulations for Fairimentals.

"That's wonderful, Tweek."

Tweek was an Experimental Fairimental. Fairimentals were powerful beings made of pure magic, guardians of Aldenmor. Tweek had been sent to Earth to help the mages.

Adriane ducked under the branches and emerged on a well-worn pathway that led to Mirror Lake. Along the shore was a row of benches where tourists could sit to observe the animals.

"I'm hungry, packleader," a quiffle complained, waddling past her on its silvery webbed feet. Opposite the benches, metal bins used for winter feedings stood in a neat row.

"It's almost summer, we don't store food here," she told the little creature.

"Ozzie does." Ozzie was Emily's special friend—an always-hungry ferret that was also a mage, although he hadn't learned what his true magical powers were yet.

Three quiffles crammed their beaks in the containers and pulled out a jumble of liver snaps, oatmeal cookies, and gumballs.

"Packmate."

Adriane smiled as a sleek black wolf abruptly materialized in front of her, white star mark gleaming on his chest. Dreamer had long since mastered turning into mist, and often moved about the forest as silent and invisible as a ghost, much to the surprise of many a woodland creature.

The warrior knelt down and placed her forehead on his, inhaling the familiar smell of her packmate as she looked into his deep green eyes.

"Packleader, our magic isn't strong like yours," a brim-bee said.

Adriane turned to the group. "You see this little blade of grass? Might not look strong, but see how it stands together with every blade in the meadow."

"*Like a pack,*" Dreamer added.

"Each of you is a warrior inside because—"

"Packmates always stand by each other," a quiffle said, puffing out his chest.

"Very good. All right, let's get started." Adriane clapped her hands sharply.

The magical animals scrambled about, falling into for-mation just as Adriane had been teaching them. The small quiffles and brimbees stood at the center, with jeeran, pegasi, and larger animals forming the outer ranks.

"Who's first?"

The animals started shouting.

"I want to try!"

"Me first!"

"I'm ready to fight!" A quiffle kicked several brimbees in mock battle.

Adriane held up her hand. "What's the first rule?"

"Focus," a wommel answered.

The animals fell silent, proudly demonstrating their concentration.

Adriane studied two wilting dogwood trees growing on either side of the benches. Their drooping branches gave her an idea. "How about we grow an archway over here?"

Cheers went up from the crowd of animals as they sat down and passed out snacks.

"Dreamer and I will start," the warrior said.

The branches would have to grow at least five feet to weave into the canopy.

With a flick of her wrist, Adriane released a small flurry of bright magic from the jewel set into a turquoise-studded leather bracelet. She sent a flash of silver deep into the cool moist earth. Dreamer responded instantly, his solid presence anchoring her. The gnarled dogwood roots seemed to reach out as Adriane pushed her magic into the trees. Bight green raced up the skinny trunks and spread into the branches, making the leaves tremble.

Then, like a ray of sunlight, Stormbringer's magic surrounded the warrior and her pack. With the power of the forest spirit, the dogwood began to grow, bark creaking, leaves rustling.

"Okay." Adriane pointed to Rasha and Roniff. "How about some dahlias around the trunks?"

The two quiffles stepped forward and waved their tail feathers, making brilliant pink flowers spring up from the rich earth.

"Nice," Adriane approved.

"Ooo, ooo, me, me!" Two overly eager brimbees tumbled forward, sending honeysuckle and rose petals fluttering through the air like confetti.

Several wommels wove a strand of silvery green magic around Tweek. Adriane smiled, helping out with a flurry of magical sprinkles. The Experimental Fairimental's quartz eyes whirled in surprise as a buttercup bow tie popped onto his neck.

"This is not authorized attire!" Tweek spluttered.

"I think you look handsome," Adriane giggled.

"Oh, thank you." The E.F. proudly adjusted his new tie.

"Now, everyone concentrate," the warrior instructed. "We're only halfway done."

Adriane closed her eyes. She gently guided the animals, helping them feel where their magic was most needed. They got into the groove, weaving the branches into a living canopy of brilliant colors.

"Almost there," the warrior breathed. The branches were only a few inches apart. Now she just had to make them entwine to support each other.

"Hey, Earth Mother!"

Adriane's eyes flew open as Kara's voice blared in her mind.

"Ahhh!"

The dogwood branches whipped back, sending fur, feathers, and hooves flying. The arch collapsed, flowers spinning everywhere.

Adriane pushed to her feet, quickly making sure the animals were all right before shooting an angry thought back to Kara. *"You ruined it!"*

"Get your roots to the library," Kara said impatiently.

"What's going on?" Adriane demanded.

"It's time."

4

"Is this it?" Ozzie, the golden-brown ferret, pointed a paw at the Ravenswood Library computer. A 3-D image of a hulking sea beast with bulbous orange eyes and large webbed feet slowly rotated on the screen.

Emily shook her head. "No, it had black fur and no scales."

"Black fur, no scales," Ozzie repeated, clicking away at his search engine.

Tweek perched on the desk next to the keyboard, tapping his twigs impatiently. "You know, if you organized your files properly, you'd have identified it already."

"I have everything just how I like it!" Ozzie snapped, adjusting the pile of pillows on his chair.

"What kind of comprehensive monster list is this?" Tweek spluttered, poking at the screen. "'Creature/horrible, creature/not so bad, creature/eats weasels.'"

"I've been working on that for months." Ozzie swatted Tweek's twigs away. He scrolled to a creature that resembled a big blob of lime Jell-O.

Emily shook her head. "No, it was more bear-like and it was wearing amulets and feathers."

"Accessorizing monsters?" Kara sat by the large curved windows that overlooked the great lawn and gardens in back of the manor. Beside her, Lyra purred as Kara vigorously brushed the cat to a golden glow.

"Tribal dress suggests intelligence and a well organized society," Tasha mused, peering behind the monitor into a muddle of cords and adapters. She was trying to hook up her jewel-tracking device to the Ravenswood computer. "It may be unidentified. The Fairy Underground has been reporting strange creatures appearing in all sectors of the web."

"The magic web is breaking down," Tweek agreed. "It's anybody's guess what portal will open where."

"A random portal in school! A creature in the library!" Adriane paced up to the computer, Dreamer at her heels. "What's next, dragonflies in French class?"

"Actually, that already happened," Kara reminded her.

"I don't think this was a random portal opening." The healer frowned, troubled. "The creature was looking for me."

"What's this?" Tweek poked a key and a file popped open.

Dear Ozzie, you are the best part of Ravens—
wood. We want you to star in our brand new
TV show. Please email back right away at—

With a click of a stick, Ozzie's file suddenly vanished.

"Gah! You deleted my email!" Orange sparks sputtered from the ferret stone on Ozzie's leather collar as he rattled Tweek's twiggy neck.

"That's it!" Emily cried, pointing to the monitor.

"You said it! Huh?" The ferret froze, back paws pressing down on several keys. Then he saw the picture of the creature he'd accidentally called up.

"Kobold. Six to eight feet tall, red eyes, amulets," Emily read the stats. "Home world, unknown. This image was recorded in the Fairy Realms a few weeks ago."

"You know, Tash," Kara said, polishing her unicorn jewel, "I was the one who got the projection to work before, but I don't even know how."

When the girls had first discovered the hidden computer in the library, it had contained a cryptic message from Ravenswood's missing owner, Henry Gardener, welcoming the mages to the magic web.

"Did you do this?" Tasha typed a command on the keyboard. The sunny library instantly became dark as the bay windows shaded over.

"Maybe."

The solar system mobile hanging from the ceiling lit up as planets and stars spun in a tight orbit. Sparkling lights cascaded along the dome, pulling together into a sprawling map. Pathways of bright stars swirled and pulsed.

"It's a map of the magic web," Kara explained. "We saw that when we first opened the computer."

"Inconceivably fantastical!" Tweek gasped. "The web is pure elegance in design," he lectured. "Magic flows along the strands, giving every realm what is needed. Where strands of the web meet, there's a portal."

"Mr. Gardener must have loaded this map before he left Ravenswood so we know the image is a few years old," Tasha figured. "And this—" The goblin sorceress tapped a key and a new image appeared across the dome.

"This is the magic web today," Tasha said proudly.

"Holy twig!" Tweek's sticks stuck out in astonishment.

Emily, Kara, and Adriane stood several feet apart, each mage looking up at the incredible display, bright lights reflecting in their eyes.

This web was completely different. What had been neatly organized was now clumped together in random patterns, large gaps appeared between strands, and some sections seemed to be missing altogether.

"Wow, how did you do that?" Emily asked.

"I've been assembling data from The Garden, the

goblin labs, warlock maps, and all of Tweek's current fairy maps."

"The entire web is falling apart!" Tweek tottered as he pointed at the ceiling. "Look! Portals are off axis, moving to where they're not supposed to be."

"Doorways to places that have been shut for hundreds of years are opening again," Tasha confirmed.

"Worlds colliding," Emily muttered.

"Why is the web shifting so much?" Kara asked.

"Simple. We're running out of magic. No magic, no web," Tweek explained.

"Unicorns are doing what they can to keep the web stable, but this is more than they can handle." Tasha pushed a sequence of keys. "Hold on to your muffins."

A small section of green enlarged. Unlike the rest of the web, it was neatly patterned, intricately beautiful like—a spider's web.

"The Spider Witch is isolated on the edge of the Fairy Realms," Tasha continued. "With the web so weak, she is simply weaving the strands into a pattern all her own. It won't be long before she re-weaves the entire web."

"What's she waiting for?" Emily asked.

"These." Tasha touched her jewel meter and three glowing points winked brightly on opposite sides of the magic web. In a sea of golden stars, the spots shone deep purple, blue, and red.

"Power crystals," Emily guessed.

"That's the good news. Here's the bad: I found them

because they're all being drawn into the witch's web," Tasha said grimly.

"Where's the fourth?" Adriane asked, searching the map for the fourth blinking light.

"I can't get a lock on it. But it's only a matter of time before it's drawn into the Spider Witch's web, too."

"We still need all *nine* power crystals," Tweek reminded them.

Kara stiffened as all eyes turned to her.

"Maybe it will work with eight," Lyra suggested.

"If you don't have all nine crystals, you can't open the Gates of Avalon," Tweek said with authority.

The blazing star's voice was calm and steady. "Any luck figuring out how to make a new crystal, Tash?"

The goblin teen shook her head, black hair swinging.

A heavy silence hung over the room. If they couldn't replace the crystal Kara destroyed, their quest to open the Gates of Avalon would fail.

"What does your crystal say about making a new one, Tweek?" Emily asked.

"No data, sorry."

"You'll figure it out, Tash," Kara said quietly.

Adriane faced the goblin sorceress. "How much time do we have?"

"Approximately none," Tasha answered. "We've got to leave right away and track down the crystals."

"Let's go!" The ferret charged, then skidded to a stop. "Wait. Where are we going?"

Tasha pulled a small pen from her robe and pointed it at the far left side of the map, projecting a pinpoint of red light. "This crystal is near Dalriada."

"That's the Unicorn Academy!" Emily exclaimed.

The goblin moved her pointer to the second crystal. It hovered around a section of the web that trailed off into blackness. "This one is in uncharted territory. The third crystal is near the Fairy Realms."

"They're so far apart from each other." The warrior studied the bright crystals on the map. "We'll never get from one point to another in time."

"It's obvious what we need to do, isn't it?" Kara arched an eyebrow.

"What?" Adriane demanded.

"Three crystals, three mages, you do the math."

The warrior narrowed her eyes. "Do you think it's smart to split up?"

"We're all pros at this. We each have paladins to protect us if things get rough. We can handle it," Kara said with confidence.

"That's not what I meant." Adriane's gaze hardened.

"Hello, we've been through this already." Kara rolled her eyes. "I helped Zach use his magic and we saved the dragon eggs. Three words: Get over it."

Adriane stepped close to the blazing star, her body tense with anger. "Why don't you just admit it was wrong?"

"What was I supposed to do?" Kara challenged. "Sit there let those dragons die?"

"Oh, you're a real team player, Kara," Adriane growled. "The whole quest to save Avalon is in danger because *you* destroyed a power crystal."

"That was an accident!" she shouted.

"Yeah, it seems you have a lot of those," Adriane snarled.

Kara's diamond jewel sparkled red. "It would just kill you to give me credit for anything, wouldn't it?"

"Stop it!" Emily snapped.

Kara and Adriane stared at the healer.

"I don't have time to play referee." Emily stood a few feet away, rainbow jewel glowing on her wrist. "If you have to fight, do it after we save the web." Her hazel eyes glinted. "We have to split up to find the crystals. But we stay in contact with each other."

"D-fly phones will keep us all in the loop," Ozzie suggested.

"Okay," the warrior said, not taking her eyes off Kara. "But no one does anything without calling the others."

"Agreed," Emily said, then turned to Kara.

The blond girl muttered, "I'd much prefer working solo than having dragon girl breathe down my neck." Before the warrior could respond, Kara picked up her unicorn jewel and sent a silent summons to the mini-dragons.

"I'll take the Fairy Realms," Emily stated. "Maybe I can learn more about the kobolds."

"I'll take Dalriada," Kara jumped in. "I need to deliver some supplies to the Unicorn Academy anyway."

"Fine. Dreamer and I go into uncharted territory," Adriane said. "Dreamer's the best magic tracker we've got."

"But we just can't leave the preserve unprotected," Emily suddenly realized.

"What am I, compost?" Tweek demanded.

"*Yes,*" Lyra confirmed.

"I'll stay," Tasha volunteered. "Zach is at The Garden guarding the crystal vault. I can monitor the web from here."

"Ariel and I will patrol day and night," Tweek promised. "Nothing will get past us!"

"A goblin, an owl, and a twig—Ravenswood is doomed," Ozzie moaned.

Adriane stood tall, wolf stone flashing on her wrist. "The animals of Ravenswood can protect themselves and the forest, I've made sure of that."

"Oh no, the tours this weekend!" Emily exclaimed.

"Great." The warrior threw up her arms. "Know any cloning spells, Tasha?"

Kara arched an eyebrow. "One of you is all I can handle, thank you very much."

Adriane made a face, silently mimicking Kara.

"Twighead can't give tours," Ozzie said, pacing the room.

"I know some people who could." Kara casually twirled her unicorn jewel.

The others stared at her blankly.

"Oh no," the warrior protested, realization dawning.

"They know the routine better than anyone," the blond girl insisted.

"Who?" Ozzie demanded.

Emily nodded, warming to the idea. "Plus they already expect Ravenswood to have a few quirks."

"Hoo?" Ariel asked.

Adriane jumped to her feet. "And what happens when a flock of quiffles starts singing to Molly and Tiffany, or a portal opens and dumps a manticore on your brother's head? They'll freak."

"Perfect," Kara giggled.

"Oh, them," the ferret grumbled.

Scowling, the warrior stalked across the library, Dreamer a dark shadow at her heels.

"So we've got our missions," Kara concluded. "Any questy-ions?"

"One more thing," Tasha advised. "You won't be the only ones tracking the crystals. Those reports of dark creatures spotted all over the web…"

"Weasel eating creatures?" Ozzie squeaked.

"Much worse." Tasha's eyes lit up. "Creatures of legend, like basilisks and chimeras and krakens are appearing for the first time in—ever. My friend in the Wildlands saw a fire-breathing worgon."

"Wow!" Tweek goggled. "What I wouldn't give to see one of those."

"Be my guest," Ozzie muttered. "You'd go up like a Yule twig."

"You must be careful." Tasha leaned forward, motioning for them to squash in close to hear her hushed voice. "These are horrible, terrible, fearsome monsters—"

Knock knock knock!

"Ahhhh!" Ozzie screamed, his fur standing on end.

"They're here!" Tweek rattled. "Save yourselves!"

"Calm down, it's only the door," Adriane said, walking slowly across the library.

Kara, Lyra, and Emily crept up behind the warrior. Adriane swung the door open, Dreamer close at her side.

"There's no one here," Emily whispered.

"Bon jour, mademoiselles."

Five mini dragons—only inches high—stood on the floor, waving their little paws. Red Fiona, yellow Goldie, purple Barney, blue Fred, and orange Blaze buzzed into the air, flapping happily around the group.

"How polite, you knocked." Kara beamed, scooping Goldie up and giving the golden d-fly a hug.

"You can make gateways between magical worlds but you can't open a door?" Adriane asked as Fred landed on her shoulder.

"I've been teaching them portal etiquette," Kara explained, petting Goldie.

"Here's the plan," Adriane instructed. "Anyone finds

a crystal, they check in with the others via d-fly. Then head straight to The Garden, where Zach will put the crystals into the vault."

The mages and their friends nodded in agreement.

"I'll guide your jumps from the Ravenswood portal to get you where you're going." Tweek was scrolling through images on his HORARFF. "But I can't promise you'll come out exactly where you need to be."

"If you get into trouble, find the nearest mirror," Tasha advised.

"Shouldn't be a problem for Kara, but what about us?" Adriane asked sarcastically.

Tweek twirled around happily. "I'm programmed with MapQuest. Tasha and I will guide you."

"Okay, I guess we're ready," Emily said. "Get whatever supplies you need and meet at the Ravenswood portal in thirty minutes."

"Everybody ready to save the universe?" Kara asked, holding her hand out.

Adriane hesitated, then placed her hand on top of Kara's.

Mages, goblin, and assorted magical beings extended hands, paws, wings and twigs, knowing the fate of the magic web and Avalon now depended on them.

5

*T*HE ENCHANTED SKY *glowed fire red as the teenagers stood within the ancient circle, their bonded animals beside them. Nine glittering crystals spun in a wash of color, binding together like pieces of a puzzle. In their center, a brilliant portal shimmered, its jewel-like surface reflecting only hints of what lay waiting on the other side.*

Dark mist coiled from the portal like curling snakes ready to strike.

But this was not the familiar magic they had used to become powerful mages. She had suspected it for some time now. Avalon would only open for one who could use the twisted power within—and she was ready to become the dark mage.

The warrior stepped forward, gem on her wrist blazing.

"What are you doing?" the blazing star demanded.

"Taking what's mine." The warrior raised her hands as the dark magic swirled around her.

Through the haze, a vision of hope appeared—her bonded animal, fiercely determined to save her. "This is not the way, bonded. If you need magic, take mine."

"I was planning to." Sickly green shot from her black jewel and wrapped around the creature.

In the blink of her bonded's shocked eyes, the dark mage did the unthinkable. In a single moment all was gone, all they had been, all they would become, wiped clean, as cold and empty as her heart.

"Why are you doing this?" the blazing star cried, horror reflected in her eyes.

"It is the only way for me now."

Before the others could stop her, the dark mage unleashed the power of Avalon.

The healer screamed as the magic ripped through her body. Even as she changed, mutated beyond recognition, her twisted fingers tried to weave the warped magic.

Desperate to save the other animals, the blazing star struck the warrior head on as chosen fought against chosen. But she was no match for the terrible power of the dark mage.

Blinding lights exploded as the crystals flew apart, tearing across the sky in jagged streaks of lightning. The Gates of Avalon vanished like a ghost.

The dark mage stood transfixed. Their quest had failed, but she had completed her path. To become a dark mage, she *had committed the ultimate act of betrayal—she had killed a bonded animal.*

And in the aftermath of destruction, what remained were nine crystals, forever tainted, gleaming with dark power...

Oily water sloshed over the seeing pool and onto the marble floor. The Dark Sorceress gasped and stepped back. For a fleeting moment, she had seen her old friends. They had been the chosen ones—mages destined to save Avalon. She had been the warrior, her sister Lucinda, the blazing star, and Silvan, the healer. But the Dark Sorceress had betrayed them all.

The images reflected in her slitted green eyes warped and vanished. Metallic nails glinted as the sorceress ran a hand through her silver, lightning-streaked hair. That had not been what she wished to see.

She had been trying to pierce the dreamcatcher guarding the portal in Ravenswood and locate the blazing star. Instead, her own hated memories had come alive in the seeing pool. How naïve they had all been to believe they could just walk right in and claim what they desired most: Avalon, the home of all magic.

Only she had possessed the foresight to recognize the real power of Avalon. Power she had coveted for so long now. It seemed like an eternity.

She passed her hand over the seeing pool, stilling the rippling waters. Once a simple exercise, using the pool had become exhausting. Constructing her new lair, maintaining its protective shield, controlling her servants—it was all taking a heavy toll. Unless she secured the magic of Avalon, she would not survive. Worse, she would never complete her transformation to the next level of magic.

The haunting visions were proof the time was at hand. The quest for the magic of Avalon was nearing completion.

This time she would be ready.

Striding from the scrying chamber, she glided down the cavernous black marble hallway. The tall lizard-guards turned, keenly observing their mistress.

She smoothed her hair and steeled her face. It was time to set the final pieces of her plan into motion. A smile stretched her blood-red lips. She no longer had any use for friends, but she understood better than anyone the advantages of using others to get what she wanted.

Stepping into the formal dining room, she spread her hands in a gesture of greeting. "Welcome to my humble keep, old friend."

A white-haired man sat at the head of a mahogany table laden with steaming dishes. On his plate were the scattered remains of a rich meal. Though age creased his rugged face, his bright blue eyes were alert. She could still see traces of the hopeful, blond boy he had been all those years ago.

"I take it the accommodations are to your liking." She swept into a seat opposite her guest.

Henry Gardener picked up his golden goblet, raising

it in salute before he sipped. "Sparkling apple ale from Farthingdale. My favorite."

Still charming, still handsome. She ignored the flare of emotion in her chest. The time had long passed when such things could affect her.

Gardener set down his goblet as a shadow passed over his eyes. "Oh, there is, however, one thing," he said, touching the collar of his elegant white shirt. "When I awoke in my luxurious suite, I realized I was not alone."

He leaned forward and loosened his collar. Along his back lay a dark, oily splotch. Spidery tentacles pierced his skin and snaked into his flesh like thick, black veins. At his touch, the black splotch moved, breathing and pulsing.

The Dark Sorceress smiled. "A shadow creature. You'll be quite comfortable as long as you refrain from using any of your tricks."

"No matter. I'll be dead in a few days unless it's removed."

"Well, you've had a very long life."

"Indeed. Haven't we all." He raised his goblet again and took a deep drink.

The sorceress sneered as long claws extended from her fingertips. "Age may agree with you, but I have no intention of feeling the years."

A sad smile formed on Gardener's lips. "All things must end, Miranda."

The sorceress laughed. "I'm sorry. You've been away.

Our old friend Silvan, or should I say the Spider Witch, has been very busy weaving a web of her own. Even as we speak it is attracting the power crystals."

His look turned stone cold. Any fleeting resemblance to the wide-eyed boy vanished. "You're both mad. Our quest is long over."

"Why? Because the Fairimentals said so?" the sorceress asked indignantly. "I would have entered the gates if they hadn't stolen our crystals."

"You betrayed us," Gardener said calmly. "You twisted the prophecy with lies."

"Even now you refuse to believe the truth. I know what you were doing when I captured you. You were searching for the crystals yourself."

"They belong to the mages. What makes you think any still hold dark power?" Gardener challenged.

She chuckled, amused. "I have already tested one. I turned the water Fairimental, Marina."

"It wasn't enough you poisoned Aldenmor!"

"The blazing star released magic to heal Aldenmor. That is how the crystals were freed."

Gardener's expression became a mixture of pride and fear.

"Your protégés have done quite well, even without you to mentor them. They have already found four power crystals. But you know as well as I do what will happen. The Fairimentals always choose three mages. And one mage always goes dark. These girls are no different. One will betray the others. That is the *real* prophecy—the prophecy of the dark mage."

Pain and worry creased Gardener's brow.

The sorceress continued, "They seek the other four crystals as we sit enjoying this lovely meal."

Gardener paused. "That's only eight. What happened to the ninth?"

"The blazing star destroyed it."

The old man flinched, watching her like a mouse caught in the serpent's stare. "What do you want from me?"

"The blazing star needs to make a replacement crystal."

"It would take years to gather the magic required to make another crystal."

"You know there is another way."

Comprehension slowly dawned upon his face. "You can't be serious."

The Dark Sorceress shrugged. "One mage will turn dark anyway. Of course, the healer or warrior could surprise us, but we both know how emotional blazing stars can be."

The blood drained from Gardener's face as the creature on his back heaved and glistened. He pushed his plate away, a sick look passing over his face.

"Keep your energy up. You're eating for two now."

Satisfaction welled inside her as Henry Gardener turned away, resignation in his pained blue eyes. The prophecy always came true.

"The mages will open the gates of Avalon, just as you

planned, Henry." The sorceress smiled evilly. "Not often we get a second chance."

"Only the chosen ones can enter Avalon," he reminded her faintly.

"We *were* chosen. I still am!" the Dark Sorceress's voice cut like steel. "Avalon's magic will be mine."

6

"*L*ooᴋ ᴏᴜᴛ!" Lʏʀᴀ pushed Kara aside as a huge duffle bag fell from the portal and thudded down beside them.

"Thanks." Kara checked the bag for damage. Goldie peered over her shoulder. This was important cargo, three hundred tubes of styling gel. "Perfect, now all we need are some unicorns."

Kara surveyed her new surroundings. She, Lyra, and Goldie stood in the center of an empty plaza where several twinkling gemstone paths converged. Behind them, a sign that read "Guest Portal" hovered above the luminous gateway.

An ornate plaque hung from a tree of gold and blue in the plaza's center.

*Welcome to the Unicorn Academy of
Dalriada. E Pluribus Hornum. May Your
Dreams Fly as High as the Sky.*

The glittering paths curved out from the plaza and through a lush meadow, each leading to enormous trees set together in shady groves. Gloriously carved entrance-ways led into hollow trunks—classrooms. A thick forest sprawled beyond the manicured meadow, amber leaves rippling in the breeze like a sea of gold.

"Unicorn U sure beats Stonehill High's campus," Kara whistled.

"But your school has students," Lyra observed, her green eyes scanning the deserted academy. There wasn't a unicorn in sight.

"Let's see if I can get anyone on the horn." She squeezed her eyes shut and sent out a telepathic message to her unicorn friends. *"Calliope, Pollo, Electra ...Ralphie? Hello?"*

No answer. Dalriada was way too quiet.

Goldie started beeping and flew to Kara's shoulder.

"Base to Star One, do you copy?" Tasha's voice magically transmitted through Goldie.

"This is Star One to Base, can you hear me?" Kara replied, speaking into the d-fly's soft belly.

"Loud can clear, Prin—, um, Star One. What's your status?"

"Arrived safely, nothing to report yet. It's strange. No sign of anyone."

"Keep us posted, Star One," Tasha said.

"Roger. Star One out." Kara gave Goldie a kiss, making the mini's faceted eyes twinkle.

Scanning the pathways, Kara spotted a large bulletin board at the entrance to several connecting trees. She walked along a rose quartz path wide enough for two unicorns to pass each other on their way to classes.

"Hmm, let's see, Hoof Care 101 has been moved to Tuesdays at ten a.m.," Kara read, studying the jumble of fliers. "Horn blowing competition, Delta Phi Horn pledge week, magic web finals study group. Where's the campus guide?"

"Here." Goldie buzzed to another board, which displayed a map of the Academy. A small horn pointed to a spot that read "You are here."

"Thanks, G-unit." Kara scanned the list of facilities. "Student union, magical supply center, playhouse, dining pools, dorms, classrooms, training fields, moonbeam ponds …"

Let's split up and cover more ground," Lyra suggested.

"Okay, Goldie, do a flyby of the classrooms. Lyra, check the dining pools, maybe they're eating lunch. I'll take the dorms."

"Right." Lyra padded away as the d-fly zipped into the air.

Kara followed a moonstone path lined with white freesias to a grove of golden trees.

Strolling through one of the doorways, she found herself in a huge round room. The hollowed out tree arched high overhead with curving golden walls. Platforms that served as beds sat on the hay lined floor.

Kara made her way across the circular dorm, noting how each unicorn had decorated its bed with personal touches. Some of the platforms were draped with garlands of fragrant wood violets, while others had brightly painted designs. Beside each platform was a flat stone piled with an assortment of combs and snacks.

She scanned the empty dorm, worried. Calliope and her unicorn buds had described the bustling Dalriada campus to Kara in many jewel-to-horn calls. Shouldn't they have seen someone by now? Something was definitely wrong here.

"Got something," Lyra announced.

"On my way." Kara sprinted across the meadow to the edge of campus.

"Look." Lyra stood beside a swath of trampled grass. A mass of hoofprints led into the forest beyond.

"A clue!" Kara exclaimed.

Walking into the woods, they rounded a bend and came upon a circular field roughly the length of a football field. Bleachers made of golden wood lined the perimeter, wide enough for the unicorns to stand and watch. It looked like an open-air stadium.

"Wow!" Kara breathed.

Upon the field, smooth stones in every shade of the rainbow formed a detailed pattern of loops and swirls. Individual stones created dozens of distinct paths throughout the larger pattern. There was something very familiar about it.

"Lyra, Goldie, let's get the aerial view," Kara called out.

Lyra soared high into the air on her glittering golden wings, Goldie flapping beside her.

"It looks like the magic web," the cat reported.

"Ah ha!" Kara nodded, her suspicions confirmed. She stepped onto a bright amethyst stone. "I wonder what kind of game they play."

Zing!

A glowing pink beach ball was suddenly hovering in front of her nose.

"Pick up your hooves, let's go!" the orb shouted in a loud, piercing voice. "Web practice is now in session."

"Huh?" Kara stared as the mysterious floating thing circled her, a pink light beam scanning the unicorn pendant.

"What kind of unicorn are you?" the ball demanded.

"I'm not a unicorn."

"You have unicorn magic," it insisted.

"I'm a mage."

"What?!" The ball sparked and whirled. "No bipeds allowed on the practice web!"

"Is that what this is?" Lyra asked, landing beside Kara.

"Ahhh!" the ball shrieked, scanning Lyra and Goldie. "No cats, no dragons, no mages, just unicorns!"

"Could you tell us where they are?" Kara asked.

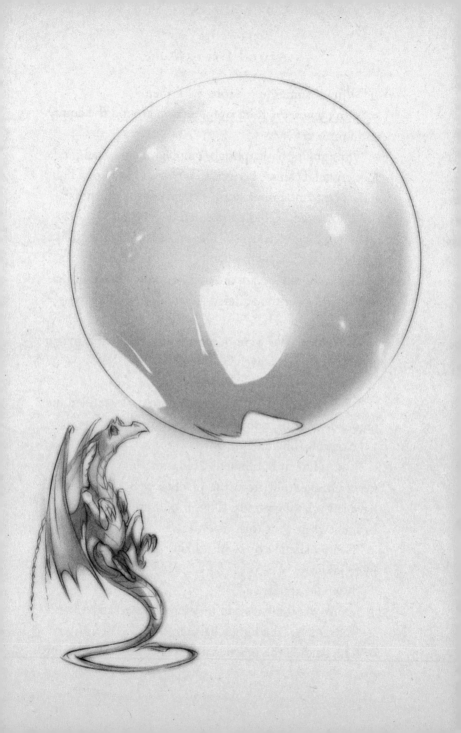

"Why, is something wrong with them?"

"Can't you see?" Kara swept an arm around the empty stadium.

"I'm a multiphasic, portal-equipped, magic web guidance crystal. I can see perfectly." It twirled in a blur of light and came to an abrupt stop. "Where are the unicorns?"

"Vamoosed," Goldie informed the crystal.

"Eaten by a vamoose?!" The orb whizzed around like a wild bee.

"Zip it, blinky," Kara ordered, sending a beam of diamond light over the agitated sphere. "When did you see them last?"

"Yesterday. We were doing exercises. Moving magic around the practice web."

"And then?" Kara prompted.

"Well, I terminated my regeneration cycle, refilled the moonbeam pools, bobbed around a bit—"

"Not you. The unicorns."

"Oh." The orb blinked. "Hmmm, logs show they never checked out from the practice web ... they must have left school grounds. Ohhhh, I'll surely get demoted to stall sweeper for this," it moaned.

"Every single one of them left?" Kara asked incredulously.

"It would appear so."

"Don't you think it's odd they haven't checked back in?"

"Extremely," the blinky ball agreed.

Kara studied the practice web. Unicorns were training

here to spread magic along the web. If something had happened to them, the web was in even greater danger than anyone knew.

"Does this thing connect to the real magic web?" she asked.

"Just locally of course."

The sphere radiated with color. In response, the practice web lit up like an amusement park. Where pathways crossed, a flare of blue shimmered in the air. Kara gasped. She had never seen so many portals in one place!

"I know what you're thinking but these portals are certainly not—" The sphere slid into the nearest portal and promptly vanished. A split second later, it appeared on the opposite side of the field, bouncing frantically. "Who left these portals open?!" it yelled.

Goldie on her shoulder, Kara paced back and forth, then suddenly whirled on the approaching ball accusingly. "Why would every unicorn in the school suddenly decide to jump a portal at once?"

"Synchronized popping is very popular—"

"Unless!" Kara held a finger up. "They were kidnapped."

"Preposterous! No one gets on the grounds without unicorn magic."

"Someone could have lured them away," Lyra suggested. *"Put them under a spell."*

"Where were they practicing yesterday?" Kara asked.

"Let's see. Second to last week of the semester … minus two… add the sunbeam … over there."

"Can you open that portal?"

"Glide this way," the sphere instructed. With a flash, a line of stones lit up, creating a bright pathway that curved between the floating blue portals. "Step on each and every stone exactly or it won't work."

With years of hopscotch behind her, Kara jumped like a pro along the glowing stones.

"I can't believe they would leave without permission," the ball bobbed.

Kara landed on the last stone in the sequence.

"I know every portal like the back of my sphere—hey, what's that?"

Before them, a large glowing gateway swirled open. A shimmering curtain of lights rippled like waves, beckoning Kara closer. She felt the familiar tingle of unicorn magic in her jewel.

"The unicorns definitely jumped through this portal," she concluded.

Through the hazy doorway, a grid of sparkling blue stretched into the distance. The power grew stronger, pulling at her dazzling jewel.

Kara gulped, a cold knot of fear in her stomach. The unicorns had all gone onto the web and none of them had returned. Whatever they'd found couldn't be good.

She turned to her crew. "We have to find out what's happened."

Lyra and Goldie nodded.

"Blinky," Kara instructed. "If we're not back in ten minutes..."

"Yes?" the orb spluttered.

"Wait another ten."

White bolts of magic crackled in the air and the portal expanded. Its surface hissed and wavered like television static as Kara, Lyra, and Goldie stepped though and vanished.

7

$\mathcal{E}$MILY BLINKED, DISORIENTED for a moment
by the wild array of creatures crowding the Fairy
Ring. Elves, pixies, sprites, boggles, and assorted gnomes
milled about, the din of their voices carrying over rows
of toadstool seats lining the open air theater. On the
ground level, a few yards away from the mirror she'd
arrived through, the rulers of all five Fairy Kingdoms
stood near ornate thrones.

"Welcome, healer."

Emily turned to see Fairy Queen Selinda making her
way through the crowd. The tall queen's sparkling wings
fluttered behind her, their rainbow swirls set off by her
pale blue dress and moonstone crown atop her honey-
blonde hair.

"I trust your journey was not unpleasant." She clasped Emily's hands.

"Fine, thank you. Tasha knows her mirrors." Emily smiled.

"I only wish the mages could visit in more pleasant times," Selinda said warmly, though her beautiful face belied deep strain and worry.

"I understand." Emily felt everyone in the ring watching them.

Selinda eyed the nervously buzzing throngs. "We have urgent matters to discuss."

"Wait for me*ooflaA*—" Ozzie's voice was cut off as two gigantic bags followed him out of the mirror, squashing the ferret flat.

"Sir Ozymandias, how goes it?" Elf King Landiwren saluted the ferret nose poking out from under a sack.

"Good, you?"

"What's all this then?" A stout goblin woman marched forward, long velvet robes billowing behind her. The Goblin Queen Raelda was a formidable force, possessing strong magic and a temper to match.

"Kara insisted on sending gifts." Emily helped the ferret to his feet.

"Ah, well, the princess has excellent taste," the woman broke into a toothy grin. "Welcome, healer mage and… um, helper mage."

Ozzie bristled but held his tongue.

"Come!" Raelda ordered.

Emily followed the queens to the center of the ring.

The crowds parted, bowing and greeting the mage. Emily caught the eye of a handsome teenage goblin with spiky black hair standing with a group of trolls: Prince Lorren. His black boots, pants, shirt, and cape accented the silver sword strapped to his waist—a very striking figure.

He bowed with a dramatic flourish, green eyes twinkling. "The lovely healer mage. Your outer beauty is matched only by the magic inside."

"Don't we look dashing," Emily playfully volleyed back. With such charm, it was no wonder the cute prince had captured Kara's attention.

A terrifyingly huge figure loomed over Emily. "What news, young mage?" Troll King Ragnar asked expectantly.

As if on cue, others now approached, all bombarding her with questions.

"How goes the quest?"

"What can you tell us about the web?"

"How long will it hold together?"

"Back off, bub!" Ozzie pushed back a giant troll toe.

Emily gulped, wishing Kara were here to deal with the crowd.

"The healer mage is under enough pressure," Raelda barked. "Let her breathe!"

But the crowd was restless, eager for answers.

"What of the fairy quakes along the borders?" a dwarf called out.

"We've seen basilisks in Winterfall!" another cried.

"Portals are opening in my attic!" a distraught gnome hollered.

Fairy Queen Selinda raised an elegant hand, instantly commanding everyone's attention. "Thanks to the blazing star, Princess Kara, the magic of the Fairy Realms remains strong—for now. But we must act quickly if the web is to be saved. Another power crystal has been discovered on the borders of our realms."

Goblin King Voraxx leaped to his feet. "If the Spider Witch gets hold of the power crystals, she will surely use them against us!"

"If she expands her web, her weaving will control the Fairy Realms," Elf King Landiwren called out.

"Alendmor and Ravenswood as well," Lorren reminded them.

Troll King Ragnar raised his ax in one huge hand. "We must secure the power crystals and storm the witch's keep now!"

The goblin prince stepped forward. "King Ragnar, the witch's lair is impenetrable, surrounded by sheer cliffs."

"We cannot move an army across those passes," King Landiwren agreed.

"The only way in is through her mirrors," Lorren concluded.

"Excellent, a stealth operation then." Ragnar rubbed thick hands together.

Lorren shook his head. "Can't be done. The mirrors Princess Kara and I used have been shut down."

"We must make a decision." Selinda's voice carried across the ring with authority. "The web as we know it has existed for centuries, and the magic has only diminished over time. With the rise of the Dark Sorceress and the Spider Witch, the magic has been depleted. It is almost gone."

Cold panic raced up Emily's spine. The extinction of magic and all she had come to love. Her worst fears realized. The full weight of her quest pressed down on her like a ton of bricks.

"Queen Selinda, there are some here who think Avalon doesn't exist anymore," a dwarf said, "that the crystal city of legends has been destroyed."

Grumblings rose from the crowd.

"We can debate the existence of Avalon all day, what we need is action!" King Ragnar raged.

"Ragnar, you know these mages have been chosen to find Avalon," the goblin queen interjected.

"The question still remains." Ragnar met Raelda's eyes with a challenging glare. "Should the mages use the power crystals to enter Avalon or do we use them against the Spider Witch and reclaim the web?"

"The only plan that makes sense is for the mages to collect the power crystals and complete their quest," Goblin Queen Raelda declared.

"Even with the remaining four crystals, that makes

only eight," King Voraxx pointed out. "They cannot open the Gates of Avalon."

"Maybe there's no magic in Avalon at all!" Dwarf Queen Praxia growled.

Ragnar nodded. "We have magic now—power crystals. Let's use that magic to defeat the witch and the sorceress!"

The crowd rumbled with agreement.

"Better to use what we have than risk everything to find a place no one's even seen in thousands of years." Troll Queen Grethal concluded.

"What say you, mage?" Elf King Landiwren turned to the healer. "Do you believe Avalon really exists?"

Emily closed her eyes. From the very first time the Fairimentals had come to her in the forests of Ravenswood, one thing had remained constant throughout her extraordinary journey—one word, one quest, one answer: Avalon.

Adriane had seen a crystal city, a vision of the past upon the mistwolf Spirit Trail. Kara had seen a mist-covered island circled by elaborate mosaic stones like a giant puzzle. Emily had been to the Gates of Avalon on a lush tropical island. It suddenly occurred to her that each of the mages had experienced something different. That meant something. But what?

Looking out at the crowd, she found all eyes trained on her. They expected her to say something important. What could she say that would make a difference?

Sensing her distress, Ozzie stepped forward, but Emily held him back.

Steeling herself she said, "I don't know what lies beyond the gates. I don't even know what Avalon is."

Voices murmured in the crowd.

She took a breath. All these people and animals were counting on her, Kara, and Adriane.

"But I do know this. The Spider Witch tried to take Ravenswood, and she failed. Ravenswood now has a new protector, strong and good. The Dark Sorceress tried to turn Marina, the water Fairimental, evil. And she failed. The Garden in Aldenmor stands strong."

The crowd listened intently.

"I used to think magic was impossible," the healer continued. "But I have met a guardian of Avalon. My paladin is the Heart of Avalon. My friends and I have been chosen to find Avalon. And I have learned that just because something *seems* impossible, doesn't mean it is. I believe there is magic in Avalon. I need you to believe with me. Because where there is magic there is hope."

The crowd cheered, heartened by Emily's impassioned words.

"I couldn't have said it better myself." Ozzie beamed up at his friend, ferret face full of pride.

"Nice, Emily," Lorren applauded.

Elf Queen Elara rose gracefully to her feet, her long, green gown fluttering in the breeze. "It is settled. The mages will gather the crystals."

"We must support the mages on their quest," Landiwren agreed.

Raelda raised her hands in the air. "Let us open the Gates of Avalon and begin anew!"

"Abomination!"

The crowd gasped as a wizened creature pushed through them and hobbled straight toward Emily. It hunched over an elegantly carved walking stick, its brown robes covering all but a yellow rat-like snout.

The creature pointed at Emily accusingly. "Opening the Gates of Avalon will unleash evil that has been locked away since ancient days!"

A gnarled paw whipped its hood away, revealing wild white hair and flashing yellowed eyes that bore into Emily with a strange fire.

The mage stepped back, shocked.

"The circle is broken," it cackled. "The last attempt to open the gates brought disaster! This time would be madness!"

Emily exchanged a worried glance with Ozzie.

The Dark Sorceress and her friends had tried to open the Gates of Avalon. What if there really was dark magic inside? That would explain why the sorceress wanted it so much.

"Step back, Olfert." Fairy King Oriel had rushed to Emily's side and spoke to the intruder. "Do not foul this fairy ring with your talk of evil legends."

"Avalon holds evil that must never be released!"

"Tell me, Olfert," Troll King Ragnar scoffed, "what evil could be worse than what we face now?"

The old mole ignored them, intent only on Emily. "Heed my words, mage. You are dealing with forces you do not comprehend. Open the gates and you shall be cursed forever!"

"That's quite enough." King Oriel reached out to grasp the cackling creature, but just as suddenly as he had appeared, Olfert vanished into the crowd.

The crowd buzzed anew as Emily stood in shock.

"Why did Olfert say Avalon's magic is evil?" she asked Lorren.

"Don't pay any mind to the ramblings of a crazy old mole," Lorren reassured her.

"The prince is right," Selinda said. "We cannot let

fear guide us. We must believe the magic of Avalon will save us."

Lorren stepped to Emily's side. "I will escort the healer mage and Sir Ozymandias on their journey to find the power crystal."

Goblin King Voraxx faced the crowd. "Our armies shall stand ready when the Gates of Avalon are opened!"

"The Fairy Realms stand united with the mages!"

"Huzzah!"

A flock of giant bats swooped over the Fairy Ring, carrying members of the Fairy Underground, a covert force led by Lorren. Two riderless bats glided down, landing next to the goblin prince.

"You take Gertie," Lorren said, pointing to Tasha's gray bat preening herself beside the prince's silver and black bat, Nightwing.

"Hi girl!" Emily patted Gertie, and the bat nuzzled her with a soft snout.

"Tasha tracked the power crystal to somewhere near the town of Dawn's Edge," Lorren told the healer. "We'll be escorted to Garion's Landing, then we go in on foot."

Taking a deep breath, Emily hopped into Gertie's saddle. Ozzie scrambled up behind her.

She searched for the mysterious Olfert. His words of warning rang in her head. But the creature was nowhere to be seen

"May the magic be with you, now and forever." Fairy Queen Selinda raised her hand in farewell as Gertie and Nightwing launched into the air.

Flying in tight V formation, twelve bats soared across the twilight sky, purple dusk slipping into the coming night.

8

"THE GIRTH ON the saddle should be snug, but not too tight. Otherwise Drake gets itchy," Zach advised, his voice magically amplified via the little blue dragonfly, Fred.

"Okay." The warrior adjusted her black boots in the stirrups, proud to be flying solo on Drake. The red dragon had imprinted on her when he'd hatched.

Adriane, Fred, Dreamer, and Drake had arrived in what Tasha labeled "uncharted territory." As far as the goblin sorceress could tell, this was not a planet like Earth or Aldenmor, but one of many magical places along the web that ended in steep cliffs or thick mist, like the Fairy Realms.

Adriane kept Drake at a low altitude as a precaution.

She had to assume there might be predatory flying creatures, and she also wanted to keep an eye out for any activity on the ground.

She scanned the jagged buttes surging from the rocky, red sand below. So far, these badlands had been nothing but a series of ridges and interconnecting canyons. Small cacti peppered the landscape and giant, bleached ribbones stuck out in stark contrast to the red ground.

"And don't feed him too much," Zach continued. "You spoil him."

"Me?" She reached forward and scratched Drake's neck. The dragon hummed with pleasure.

"Only 200 pounds a day," Zach warned.

"He must be on a diet," Dreamer snorted, leaning forward in his wicker basket secured to the back of the saddle.

"I packed Drake's favorite wheat noodles, just like you told me." Adriane patted the saddlebags hanging behind Dreamer's basket.

"He likes them with extra Ak sauce."

"I know."

"And he drinks about twenty gallons of water a day."

"We'll be fine, Mr. Mom."

The dragon huffed a puff of smoke, a dragonish chuckle.

Suddenly Dreamer perked up, nose high in the air. *"Over those rocks."*

The wolf had been having trouble tracking the power

crystal. It seemed to be appearing and disappearing at random. But now he had locked onto the crystal's magical scent moving northeast at a constant speed.

Fred hiccupped a loud burst of static into Adriane's ear and the connection to Zach wavered.

"Why can't we use our own jewels to communicate with each other?" Zach asked.

"Too risky. I've been tracked before from jewel transmissions. You got a problem with Barney?"

"He's cool, just a little smaller than what I'm used to." There was a brief pause.

"What?" Adriane prompted.

"I'd rather talk to you in person."

Adriane blushed, the wind prickling her hot cheeks. "You just hold down the fort."

Sometimes she wished Zach lived on Earth instead of Aldenmor so she could see him every day. But Aldenmor was the only home he'd ever known. The teen had grown up with his mistwolf brothers and sisters, protecting their world. He had stayed behind at his new home, The Garden, to guard the vault that contained the power crystals the mages had already found.

"Check in every hour."

"Promise." Adriane grinned.

"Bye, Zach!" Drake trumpeted happily to his bonded.

"Over there, warrior." Dreamer pointed his nose toward the ridgeline.

Adriane straightened her flying goggles, thankful

she had taken Zach's advice and packed them. She was warm enough in her black tank-top even though she had packed her jacket. Her body, lean and toned from years of running, sat comfortably in the saddle. She held the reins lightly, giving Drake enough room to keep his speed without jostling his riders.

"Take us in, Drake."

Feeling the tap of her right boot, the dragon soared in a wide arc, picking up speed as his wings caught the dry updrafts rising from the cliffs below.

"We're not the only ones here." Adriane leaned forward as the mighty dragon cleared the ridgeline. Blackened campfires spread over the low-lying hills, their smoky remains a sure sign that someone—a lot of someones—had recently been here.

"Wolf Fire to Base," Adriane spoke into Fred's blue belly.

"Copy, Wolf Fire. Go," Tasha's voice responded.

"We've spotted the remains of several encampments," the warrior reported as they flew into the canyon.

"This is so exciting!" Tweek's voice cut in. "You're in a whole new quadrant of the web! I'm extrapolating!"

Fred let out a few beeps and boops, the sound of Tasha adjusting her magic meter. "The power crystal is dead ahead, but I'm getting some very strange readings. Stay alert, Wolf Fire, you're probably not the only ones after that crystal," the goblin advised.

"Roger, Base." Adriane
paused. "What's new from
Star One and Doctor D?"

"So far, so good. They're
both on the trail of crystals."

"Okay, Wolf Fire out."

Drake soared over another canyon, the largest one
Adriane had seen so far. Dust devils spun in the deep
basin, obscuring the eerie landscape with shimmering
reds and golds.

The mistwolf growled in sudden alarm. *I've got
something!*

"Where, I don't—"

The sky exploded in fire.

Dreamer howled as Drake staggered in mid air.
Adriane responded instantly, hauling the reins tight and
forcing the dragon's eyes away from the blast.

Something whizzed by Adriane's head. An arrow, flam-
ing with bright blue magic! A split second later, another
arrow trailed vivid light across the sky. Several more deto-
nated like fireworks, shooting across Drake's wings.

The ground tilted crazily as the dragon fought for
control, roaring in pain.

Another volley whistled dangerously close.

"Base! We're under attack!" she yelled, then realized Fred had disappeared.

The warrior raised her right wrist, jewel blazing as she struggled to guide Drake through a maze of exploding magic.

"Dive! Dive! Dive!" she commanded.

Wings folded, the dragon plunged straight toward the ground.

"Hang on, Dreamer!" Adriane shouted. Silver fire streaked through the air, disintegrating dozens of arrows.

The mistwolf hunkered low in the basket, hackles raised.

"Now!" Adriane shouted.

At the last minute, Drake extended his wings, skimming the ground like a red rocket.

Groups of heavily armored lizard-like creatures swarmed into the canyon.

"Magic hunters," Adriane spat.

Drake swept overhead, roaring fire and scorching the ground. In a flurry of screams, the hunters ran off in all directions.

"Easy." Adriane pulled the reins left, sweeping Drake in a tight circle.

Whipping her arm, she flung rings of fire around the hunters.

They threw down their weapons as the silver magic crackled fiercely against the red sand. Her message was received loud and clear: Don't mess with us!

"They're after the power crystal," Dreamer said.

"Good luck, chumps!" Adriane waved at the hunters as Drake zoomed away, adding a powerful roar of agreement.

"Something smells." The mistwolf sniffed over Drake's flank.

"I took a bath before leaving The Garden," Drake insisted.

"The power crystal?" Adriane asked.

"Yes, up ahead in the next valley," Dreamer confirmed. *"But there's something else."*

The warrior's wolf stone blazed deep red.

She gripped the reins tightly and leaned low against Drake's neck. "Okay, let's do it."

The red dragon caught an updraft. With a powerful beat of wings, they crested the ridgeline and dove into the wide valley. Before them, thick coils of purple smoke whirled, glints of light sparkling inside.

"What is that?"

"Power crystal!" Dreamer howled.

The smoky coils thrashed as if alive, snaky threads twisting into a shape with venomous eyes and gleaming teeth.

This wasn't just smoke. It was some kind of creature. Adriane raised her wolf stone as the monstrous apparition turned burning eyes to face her.

Fear ripped through her, deep and fierce. She was falling, caught in a vortex of shadow and smoke, the air knocked from her lungs, helpless. Sharp panic seized her heart. All she wanted to do was run away. She gasped, but didn't have breath to scream as blackness engulfed her—she was a little girl lost and alone in the dark, no one was coming for her, no one would find her. Pure fear wrapped around her tighter and tighter, her throat constricting until she knew she would drown in absolute terror.

Then suddenly it stopped.

Adriane found herself on the ground, dust blowing over her sweat-soaked body, a wolf howl ringing in her head.

Beside her, Dreamer snarled, hackles raised, saliva frothing from his mouth.

Adriane scrambled to her packmate. Ignoring his snapping teeth, she cupped Dreamer's head firmly. "It's okay. You're okay now."

Dreamer calmed, hanging his head low. *I was alone with no packmate.*

"That will never happen, you hear me?" She looked deeply into the wolf's green eyes.

Drake's huge head swung over Adriane's shoulder protectively.

Mama!

Adriane stroked the dragon's head, scratching just above the eye ridges.

"It's okay, I'm here now."

The dragon sat on the sandy ground with a thump, sending a cloud of dust skyward.

"What was that thing?" Adriane shuddered.

In a burst of twinkly blue, Fred appeared and dove into Adriane's arms. "Adee!"

"Oh geez, Fred!" The warrior hugged the little dragon as Dreamer leaned in close. Drake's wings folded over them, completing the group hug.

"Much better, Team Wolf." She ran her hand over Drake's flank, checking for wounds. It seemed his thick dragon hide had protected him.

"I was scared," Drake said.

"Yeah," Fred squeaked.

"Me too." Adriane anxiously scanned the landscape. Wind and sand had sculpted ancient rocks into strange, looming shapes. Cliff walls in the distance created narrow shadowy passages.

But the monster was gone. And it had taken the power crystal with it.

"Any scent on the crystal?" she asked Dreamer

He sniffed the air. *"No. It's gone—"* the wolf abruptly snapped to attention, a growl buzzing in his throat.

From behind a jutting rock several hundred yards away, wide purple eyes stared at them in astonishment.

"I don't believe it!" Adriane gasped. "It's a—"

With a swift movement, a giant jet-black creature stepped into view. Its long neck, horse-like head and shimmering scales were unmistakable. Lifting its sleek head, the creature opened immense shimmering wings and roared.

"Dragon!" Drake finished.

9

"We're not in Podunk anymore."

Kara , Lyra, and Goldie walked along a wide blue and green pathway. Colorful highways of light looped and swirled around them as far as they could see, forming the intricate pattern of the magic web.

Kara stomped her boots, testing the solidness of the glittering path. Magic thrummed through her, moving beneath her feet to places she could only imagine—and some she couldn't.

Looking closely at the strands, Kara frowned. The surface was torn and faded in spots, like fabric that had frayed. In the distance, sections had crumbled completely, leaving huge gaps. Pieces of web unraveled, strands drifting like loose threads.

She had been on the web several times before, the last time astride the white unicorn on a mad mission to save Aldenmor, but she had never seen the web in such bad shape.

"Wow, how can the web be so flooie this close to Dalriada?"

Her stomach fluttered with anxiety. It was the unicorns' job to run the web, spreading magic. If the web was this bad here, then how bad off was it everywhere else?

There was no sign of the unicorns or their magic—but there was something else.

Sparkles flickered across Kara's face as her unicorn jewel flashed bright red. She felt a familiar pull—unmistakably strong magic.

"Power crystal!" she whooped. "Over on one of those strands, I can feel it!"

Goldie buzzed to Kara's ear, stopping the blazing star in her tracks.

Tasha's staticky voice cried, "Base to Star One, come in Star One!"

"Hi, I'm on the web," Kara replied.

"Incredifulous!" Tweek crackled excitedly.

"No biggie. We're right outside Dalriada."

"No, you're not," Tasha exclaimed. "You just jumped clear across the web from Dalriada!"

"We don't know where the twig you are!" Tweek screamed joyfully.

Kara stopped short. "I thought you said the power crystal was near Dalriada."

"It is … was …" Tasha said, confused.

"You're probably picking up crystal residue from the portal we just used." Kara scanned the web, her internal radar switching to danger mode.

"Brilliant energy flux theory," Tweek approved. "I'm triangulating the portal shifts."

"Got the PC, Star One," Tasha broke in. "You're practically right on top of it. It's just sitting there."

Suddenly a wave of magic rushed through Kara. Brilliant colors sparkled behind her eyes, as if she were connected to the crystal already. And its power was beyond glorious.

"Hey," Kara suddenly realized. "I bet the power crystal lured the unicorns here!"

"Aren't the unicorns at the academy?" Tasha asked.

They're all missing," Lyra reported.

Emily's concerned voice popped in. "What do you mean missing?"

But Kara barely heard them. The magic of the power crystal tingled from her toes to her nose.

"Kara, you have to find the unicorns," Emily insisted. "I have a feeling something terrible has happened."

"Power crystal first, unicorns second. Comprende? We're wasting time, Star One out!" Kara shouted.

She poked Goldie in the belly to hang up.

"Pfft!" the d-fly squeaked.

Kara huffed as she strode down the green-tinged pathway. There was a power crystal at stake here and she wasn't going to let it slip through her fingers. This was her chance to prove to everyone she could do it right! And if the whole unicorn population really was in trouble, Kara was going to need some back-up magic anyway.

"Sorry, G-fly." She scratched Goldie's head as the mini settled on her shoulder.

Lyra trotted beside her. Kara could tell her bonded was disturbed. She hoped Lyra wouldn't say anything.

"Emily has a special connection with unicorns," Lyra said gently.

"So do I." Kara stopped, spreading her arms wide. "Do *you* see them anywhere?"

"No."

"But the crystal is right here. Maybe it isn't moving because someone else is about to grab it, huh, huh? Did anyone think about that?"

"Still, the unicorns could be in danger."

"I bet the extra magic of a power crystal can help us find them," Kara pointed out.

"That makes sense," Lyra agreed.

"Good." Kara felt better until she looked down. She lifted her boot and gasped.

"Ewww!" Goldie winced. "Gummy boot."

Green slime stuck to the polished heel of her tan leather boots.

"My new Renaldos!"

Lyra padded gingerly ahead, her paws sticking to a thin layer of green slime. *"It's all over."*

Kara tiptoed along the strand, getting as little of her boots in the guck as possible. But the ooze was getting thicker, clinging like—

Kara bent down to examine the substance. "I know this ick!"

Vivid memories of escaping the Spider Witch's lair with Lorren flew through her mind.

Lyra tensed. *"We're on the Spider Witch's web."*

Kara studied the web closer. Unlike the weaker strands of the old web, this section was tightly woven, green light pulsing ominously along a thick spidery pattern.

"Look!" Goldie pointed her wingtip over the path's edge.

Another strand gleamed a few feet below them. Stuck to its surface was a large green cocoon, dripping with slime. Something blue glowed inside.

Raising her arms, Kara sent tendrils of pink light snaking from her fingertips. As her magic reached through the webbing, she was rewarded with a charge of pure power. Her jewel lit up like a sparkler.

"You found it!" Kara exclaimed as Goldie somersaulted happily in the air.

Kara leaped over the edge and landed on the strand below, Lyra right behind her.

"I don't like this." The cat growled low in her throat, shaking bits of goo from her fur. *"I smell trouble."*

"Don't be a 'fraidy cat." Kara pointed a finger at the cocoon, projecting a thin laser beam of twinkling red light. "Can you believe it? We're the first ones to find a power crystal! How cool is that? I sure wish it's the best, most beautiful crystal ever found by mage, cat, or D-unit!"

With a few deft slices of Kara-magic, the sticky green webbing began to fall away. Magic flared like wildfire, streaming from the center of the webbing. When the glow subsided, Kara gazed at her outstretched hands.

"Whoa."

In her palms was the most amazing gem she had ever seen. It was an exact duplicate of the unicorn-horn shaped jewel that hung from her neck. Except it was three times the size.

"It looks like your unicorn jewel," Lyra observed, gazing warily at several strands of web slowly shifting toward them.

"But it's bigger." Kara smiled as pink, silver, red, gold, and diamond white swirled around the gem's smooth surface with iridescent sparkles. All her favorite colors in one fantabulous jewel. "And better!"

Lyra studied the gem uneasily. *"We already found a unicorn power crystal in New Mexico."*

"Maybe there are two of them." Kara clutched the radiant crystal ecstatically. Warm magic engulfed her, filling her with the most joyous feeling of accomplishment. "It's the best power crystal ever!"

Lyra's ears twitched nervously. *"Let's call Tasha and Tweek. We need to take it back to The Garden."*

"I thought you wanted to find the unicorns," Kara reminded the cat.

Suddenly they heard a faint hissing.

"What's that?" Kara looked up sharply, her jewel pulsing with danger.

Lyra tensed, a deep growl rumbling in her throat. The hissing grew louder. It was all around them.

With a roar, Lyra slammed into the blazing star.

Kara tumbled aside just as a gigantic purple spider dropped from the web above. It missed her by inches. The hideous creature raised up on its back four legs, sharp mandibles snapping at the air with deadly force.

Goldie fluttered in the air, spitting tiny flames at the spider's head.

Blazing magic lashed from Kara's fists as she sprang to her feet. In an explosion of light the spider was blown off the web and disappeared into the void.

More spiders advanced, swinging in on strands of green web, clicking and clattering in a sickening insect orchestra.

Snarling, Lyra crouched low, ready to defend her friends.

Kara clutched the power crystal tightly. Diamond white magic flowed from her hands, spreading out in waves. "Stay close."

"Behind you!" Lyra growled.

The blazing star spun as hundreds of spiders charged from every direction, red eyes glowing.

"Finders keepers!" Kara threw a fiery red shield around Lyra, Goldie, and herself.

The spiders swarmed onto the shield, clawing and spitting green ooze. Kara shuddered at the gruesome sight, but her magic shield held strong. The spiders were no matches for a Level Two blazing star armed with a power crystal.

That didn't stop them from trying. Ear-splitting shrieks echoed inside the bubble as waves of spiders covered the dome in sticky green goop. All Kara could see was a mass of legs, oozing fanged mouths, and livid red eyes.

"I hate bugs!" Kara cried.

Lyra swished her tail. *"Well, now what?"*

"Why is it," Kara asked, as spiders continued to pile onto the shield, burying them in a revolting mass, "that *we* always end up somewhere gross?"

Goldie preened the ick from her delicate wings. "Pukey."

"Just once," the blazing star continued, "I wish this quest would take us to the most wonderful place ever!"

In a flash of dazzling light, Kara, Lyra, and Goldie vanished.

10

*M*OSS-DRAPED TREES HUNG over snaking streams as Emily, Lorren, and Ozzie hiked through the marshy outback. All was quiet save for the wind rustling through reeds and the occasional birdcall or croaking frog. They were about a mile from the small town of Dawn's Edge, where the Fairy Underground had dropped them off. There hadn't been much to the outpost, just a stable, supply store, and a few grizzled spriggans who collected rare local herbs. It was the last trace of civilization before the Fairy Realms ended in a wall of thick, mysterious fog.

"Lorren, do you really think there's dark magic inside Avalon?" Emily followed the tall goblin prince along a meandering dirt path. Ozzie sat atop her backpack, chewing a slab of turkey jerky.

"Olfert is just a doomsayer," Lorren scoffed. He frowned as he saw the worry in Emily's eyes. "What is it?"

The healer shivered as moisture clung to her red curls. "It's just that the Dark Sorceress told me *she* tried to open the Gates of Avalon. I mean, it makes sense that she'd want dark magic."

Lorren hesitated. "Most believe Avalon is good. There's always a few who say it doesn't even exist. Then there are those, like Olfert, who think Avalon holds dark magic."

Ozzie threw his paws in the air, sending his turkey jerky flying. "How many legends are there?"

"Plenty." Lorren whacked away thick berry vines. "Most are just stories every kid hears around the campfire."

"Fairy tales," the healer smiled.

Lorren arched an eyebrow. "Nobody can say for certain what's hidden there, but everyone agrees on one thing. We need nine power crystals to find out."

They walked in silence, listening to a lone whippoor-will's call.

Lorren noticed Emily's troubled expression. "What about your speech? I thought you believed in Avalon."

Emily shook her head, confused. "I do. But with magic, anything is possible."

Lorren glanced at Ozzie. "Didn't the Fairimentals tell you about the legends of Avalon?"

"No." The ferret frowned, clearly disturbed.

"They never said anything about opening the gates?"

"No."

"What about anyone else who tried to open—"

"Gah! The Fairimentals didn't tell me anything about Avalon!" Ozzie burst out. "I was supposed to find three mages and go home, that's all."

Emily sensed a sharp flare of pain from her friend. She had been so wrapped up in herself, she hadn't stopped to consider what Ozzie was going through. This quest had literally transformed him, ripping him away from his life as an elf on Aldenmor. It occurred to her that for all her powers to see magic, she had never seen Ozzie as he truly was.

As if reading her mind, Lorren explained, "Dawn's Edge was once a beautiful area the elves called home. That was way back when they actually practiced magic."

"I didn't know that, Ozzie," Emily said. The elves of Aldenmor didn't use magic, unlike the elves that lived in the Fairy Realms.

"Most of the elf population moved to Aldenmor and took up more practical lifestyles like farming, leather making, and dumpling rolling," Ozzie told her.

"Guess you're the exception." Lorren pointed to his ferret stone.

"Yeah, a regular wizard of Ozzie," the ferret groused. "I'm just a helper-mage who can talk loud and break wind. That comes in really handy when you're trying to save the entire web."

Emily understood how frustrating it was to have magic and not know what to do with it. "The Fairimentals chose you for a reason," she assured him.

Ozzie hopped down from Emily's backpack, grumbling, "Probably because every other elf on Aldenmor had something more important to do."

"So what were you like before you were sent to Earth?" Lorren asked.

"Taller." The ferret sighed and kicked at a cattail.

After the mages had healed Aldenmor, the Fairimentals offered to turn Ozzie back into an elf. He could have gone home to his village in Farthingdale, gone back to his life. But he had chosen to help the mages at Ravenswood, which meant staying in a ferret's body. Emily often wondered how much that choice had cost him.

"Ozzie, what do you miss most about being an elf?" the healer asked softly.

"Besides having opposable thumbs?" A smile played on the ferret's furry lips. "There's nothing I loved more than the Crabapple Fair at harvest time. My, er, friend, Esmerelda, and I, would wigjig until midnight, eating bubbleberry pie as the moons rose."

"You never told me that. It sounds wonderful," the healer said.

"I was supposed to be a farmer, like my parents and grandparents. I never really wanted to do that. There had to be more to life than rutabagas." He looked away.

"I was sent to find you and Kara and Adriane. What if I already did everything I'm supposed to do?"

"If your mission was truly over, why did the Fairimentals give you a magic jewel?" Emily asked.

Ozzie touched the orange gem with his paw. "How should I know?"

"You're a Knight of the Circle," Lorren reminded him.

"An honorarium from some dumb old club. I might as well be Count Chocula."

"I have such amazing friends," Emily stated. "Lorelei, Kara, Adriane, Indi. And I wouldn't have met any of them without you." She knelt and looked Ozzie in the eye. "But you know what?"

"What?"

"*You* are my best friend." She gave the ferret a big kiss on his furry head. "You take care of me. I take care of you."

"All right, all right," Ozzie mumbled, embarrassed. "Nothing more pathetic than a wet ferret."

Rrrring!

In a burst of twinkles, Fiona popped onto Emily's shoulder.

"Base to Doctor D, come in!" Tweek's agitated voice echoed from the d-fly.

"Calm down, Tweek, what's going on?" the healer asked.

"I'm picking up massive magical flux ahead of you!"

"The power crystal?" Emily asked anxiously.

"Most likely. I can't be sure and Tasha's out checking on the animals. The place is crawling with tourists."

"You just stay put and don't let anyone in the library," Emily advised.

"Don't worry, I'll wear a hat."

"Kara's friends can handle it," Emily assured him.

"Oh, that reminds me, Kara's missing," Tweek informed her calmly.

"What???" Emily, Ozzie, and Lorren exclaimed.

"She disappeared from the web, but she didn't use any portal I can track."

"Any word on the unicorns?" Emily asked nervously. Not being able to sense Lorelei made her very uneasy. It felt like a tiny piece of her was missing.

"Negative, but I'll let you know as soon as I hear anything," Tweek said. "Over and out."

"Don't worry," Lorren smiled. "The princess has more magic than anyone I know. And if that doesn't work, she'll charm her way out of trouble."

Ozzie snorted.

"Kara's powerful all right," Emily agreed.

"She's amazing!" Lorren's cheeks blushed dark green. "I don't know how she does everything she does."

Amazing, Emily thought. Kara should have been trying to find the unicorns, but once the blazing star's mind was made up, no one could change it. Sometimes she was too powerful for her own good. It had gotten her into trouble more than once. No use pointing that out to Lorren, Kara's biggest fan.

The goblin prince paused at a crossroads. Two trails ran in opposite directions, obscured by billowing mist. "This is the end of the Fairy Realms. People who wander too deep into those mists don't usually report back."

Ozzie squinted into the fog. "Which way?"

Emily's head swam as her rainbow jewel cycled through red, green, and purple.

"Where is that magical flux Tweek was warning us about? I can't see a thing," Lorren complained.

"There's something out there." Emily could feel it, tingling like goose bumps up her back.

"Can you track the power crystal?" Lorren asked.

Ozzie gazed up at Emily, a silent question in his deep brown eyes. He knew she could see the crystal with her Level Two powers.

When Emily became a Level Two mage, she had learned how to actually see magic. Unlike Kara and Adriane, Emily could look at an animal or mage and see a colorful magical aura glowing around them, each one as unique as a thumbprint. And that was only the beginning of her powers. If she desired, Emily could take that magic and use it for herself. She had learned the hard way that could have dire consequences. The Dark Sorceress had tricked Emily, manipulating the healer into stealing magic from the animals of Aldenmor. Their screams still haunted her.

Looking down at her brave friend, Emily thought of all he had sacrificed in the quest for Avalon. There was only one right thing to do.

Steeling herself, Emily took a deep breath and closed her eyes. She visualized her own swirling rainbow aura and then Ozzie's orange golden glow. She paused, noting that Lorren, though not a mage, had a faint silver glow around him.

Gingerly, she expanded her vision into the mist. A world of glowing magic blossomed in her mind's eye. Flashes of fur, snouts, whiskers, and flippers rushed through her mind. Their auras swirled in a beautiful kaleidoscope, each one reaching out as they sensed the healer's magic. Emily skimmed over the eager animals, careful not to touch them.

She spotted a concentration of reddish magic just ahead and her pulse quickened. "I found something."

It found her, too. Suddenly she was enveloped in the bright red power. It reached out for her, calling to her. The magic was fierce—and familiar.

"Power crystal?" Lorren asked.

"No." Her eyes flew open. "Kobolds."

After connecting with the kobold in the school library, its magic was forever imprinted upon her rainbow jewel.

"Where?" Ozzie asked.

Emily gulped. "Everywhere."

Dozens of red eyes gleamed through the swirling fog. Hulking creatures with black fur came into focus, amulets of feathers and pointed teeth hanging on their thick necks.

"Stay close," Lorren whispered.

Ozzie stood in front of Emily protectively.

One kobold stepped forward, a dark shadow against the pale mist. It was the same creature who'd come to Emily in the library! A sharp-toothed grin split its face.

To Emily's surprise, the other kobolds abruptly stopped and fell to their knees.

"Dark witch." The leader bowed his head.

He gestured, and two others hurried forward and set an ornately carved onyx box at Emily's feet.

"We bring you an offering," the leader said, raising the lid.

A hissing mass of spiders swarmed from the box. Their shiny red and black legs clicked as their glowing green eyes locked onto Emily. The healer scrambled back, disgusted.

"Bugs!" Ozzie leaped into Lorren's arms.

Without even thinking, Emily waved her hand. Instantly, the spiders froze.

The kobolds gasped appreciatively.

The leader clasped his hands together. "Thank you for answering our call, great web weaver."

"Web weaver?" Lorren sounded surprised.

Emily stopped cold, remembering what the Dark Sorceress had told her. The Spider Witch had been a healer once. She and Emily used the same kind of magic. That's why the kobold had come to her in the library.

"They think I'm the Spider Witch," she whispered.

"That's crazy," Lorren said.

"I can weave magic like she does."

"But how do they know that?" Ozzie asked, eyeing the kobolds suspiciously.

The leader called out. "Great witch, terrible magic has destroyed our home!"

"Thanks for the bugs but we're on important mage business." Ozzie grabbed Emily and slowly backed up.

The kobold looked distressed. "No one else can help us."

Lorren edged close to Emily and whispered. "The crystal Kara found sure messed up the Fairy Realms."

Emily nodded and addressed the kobolds. "We will help you."

The kobolds smiled, sharp teeth shining.

Ozzie eyed the fierce creatures warily, not knowing if they were pleased or getting ready to eat them. "Listen up, you things." He puffed out his chest, ferret stone sparking. "If you even think about hurting this healer, you'll have to go through me first."

"You will not harm us." Emily pinned the creatures in her gaze, her rainbow stone glinting with the strength of her magic. "Take us to your home."

The large leader warned, "Prepare yourself. You've never seen a more terrible, awful, disgusting place."

"I guess you haven't been to Bernie's Boar and Grill," Ozzie quipped.

The kobolds parted, making a path for Emily, Ozzie, and Lorren. "The way lies through the deep mist."

The kobold leader guided them along a rough trail. The fog became thicker the farther they went. On either side, misty mountain walls loomed, closing in around them like a giant maw.

"Here." The kobold leader stepped through a glowing patch of mist and disappeared.

Lorren frowned. "Another drifting portal."

"The crystal is in there." Emily peered nervously into the gleaming mist. Would she be able to handle what lay on the other side?

"We're with you," Ozzie assured her.

She smiled gratefully. Whatever this awful place turned out to be, she, Lorren, and Ozzie would deal with it.

Emily marched after the kobolds. Gray mist surrounded her, thick and suffocating, as if they were walking through murky water. Suddenly the fog vanished and she was standing in bright clear sunlight.

The kobolds wailed, shivering with fear.

Emily stared at the unbelievable vista before her, barely able to speak. "Oh... my..."

"Gah!"

11

"**L** OOK AT THIS place!" Kara whirled around, trying to take in everything at once.

The blazing star, Goldie, and Lyra had materialized on a wide promenade. Dozens of boutiques with windows tinted pink, purple, and green circled a splashy fountain of dancing waters. Jumbo screens flashed holographic ads against a pastel dome.

"She's here!" A small purple spriggan twirled toward her, waving his arms excitedly.

As if on cue, a musical fanfare soared through the air with a dramatic flurry of bells and horns. Hundreds of excited fairy creatures tumbled out of storefronts, converging on Kara in a wave.

"Where are we?" Kara asked, startled by her welcome.

"Exactly where you want to be!" Three frog-like boggles wearing red tuxedos appeared behind her, nearly crying with joy.

"You have arrived in the greatest place on the web," the first boggle declared.

"The Fashion Realm!" the second boggle cried proudly.

Kara's eyes widened. "The Fashion Realm?"

"The best mall in the universe!" the crowd chorused.

"YippEE!" Kara squealed.

Colorful pixies and sprites swarmed around the blazing star. "We are here for you."

"And you." A silver sprite waved at Lyra.

"You, too." A tiny green fairy pointed to Goldie.

Kara paused. "How did we get here?" she demanded of the fairy creatures.

Just a minute ago, she'd been buried in gross spider gunk. And now she was in, without a doubt, the most awesome place on the web. Definitely weird.

The boggles bowed. "Your wish is our command."

Kara glanced at the amazing unicorn-shaped power crystal in her hands. The bright jewel swirled as if alive, responding to her every touch.

"What magic!" A pack of purple pixies flitted around Kara. "Let us bathe in your brilliance."

Kara beamed, running a hand through her blonde tresses. "Ew."

Her hair was streaked with dried spider goop, her suede jacket and jeans stained green.

Lyra shook her rear foot and growled at her muck-matted fur.

"We need a bath." Goldie wrinkled her little nose, pulling icky strands from her wings.

Kara sighed. "I wish there was a salon here."

Suddenly every fairy, pixie, spriggan, and sprite broke into dance. Like spinning tops, blazing star and blazing bondeds were ushered into a glorious salon and plopped into three custom sized shampoo chairs. Carrying arm-loads of supplies, the fairy creatures burst into song:

Welcome, welcome, welcome,
we all know who you are

A goddess of magic, the blazing star
We'll pamper, polish, primp, and preen
A princess you are, but you'll look like a queen

"Now this is what I call customer service," Kara approved as a delighted fairy flew up and offered her a frosty glass. "Mmmm, my fave, raspberry lemonade."

Dozens of sprites gently massaged her scalp, shampooing and conditioning her hair in a flurry of sweet smelling bubbles.

Nothing's too good for the fairest of the fair
From painted toes to shiny hair

"Manicure, pedicure?" Two impeccably dressed sprites swooped to her side with a basket of pink nail polish, files and buffers. They beamed at Goldie and Lyra. "Wingicure, clawicure?"

The unicorn power crystal sat on the sink, pulsing hypnotically, bathing Kara's face in swirling pink light. That's odd, she thought dreamily, didn't I just put that in my pocket?

"*Only Kara gives me a bath!*" Lyra tried to shake off the pixies rubbing and scrubbing at her.

"These fur care products are 100 percent organic from the purest natural botanicals, flowers, fruits and berries," a blue pixie told the cat.

"Really?"

"Rose scented, too."

"Excellent!" Kara yelled.

In her little chair, Goldie sat wrapped in a tiny robe, watching her wing tips and claws being polished and painted sunshine gold. The sprites sized up her cowlick before giving it a deftly designed clip.

The swelling chorus filled the salon over the hum of the blow dryers.

> *With your magic you can go far*
> *You're more than a star*
> *You are a blazing superstar!*

Rainbow light sparkled as Kara spun out of the salon, smiling and waving to her adoring fairy fans. Her beautiful face appeared on the jumbotron screens throughout the mall, lustrous hair swirling, shining, and rippling in golden waves around her.

"She's energized, sparkilized, and dancersized!" the boggles chanted, applauding.

Lyra ran after her. *"Kara, shouldn't we be heading back?"*

But Kara was in the groove, dancing with the crowd through the mall.

> *There's so much to do before we can stop*
> *Now that you're spritzed, you can shop, shop, shop!*

"Lyra!" Kara suddenly screamed.

With a ferocious roar, Lyra leaped to her bonded, ready to protect her. *What is it?*

"Look!"

Colorful signs adorned every storefront:

TODAY ONLY, BLAZING STARS TAKE 99% OFF!

"Grrrrr!" Lyra grrrred. *You're under a shopping spell.*

Then she saw it.

"Blingo."

Kara rushed inside the boutique directly in front of her. In the window floated a knee-length, crimson satin dress with tiny rhinestone stars glittering along the hem. It was so beautiful she thought she would cry. How amazing would she look wearing this to the school dance?

But wait! Next to that was another even more perfect outfit. A jade jersey halter dress and next to that was a scarlet ruched taffeta dress and jackets with fur trim—

"Stop the spell!" Kara commanded in a blaze of jewel bits.

The music echoed away as she examined the collar closely. "Is that faux fur?"

"Of course," the shop spriggan answered. "The finest in synthetics."

"All righty, then," Kara beamed, then frowned. "Does this come in my size?"

"What do you wear?"

"Four."

"They're all size four!" the spriggan cried.

"Woo-hoo!" Kara yelped, stomping around Lyra.

Goldie joyfully somersaulted over Kara. "Do you have anything in a size .02?"

"Absotootly!" The spriggan beamed.

"Ooo, I can't decide." Kara skipped from store to store.

"Kara!" Lyra bolted after the blazing power shopper.

A dozen dwarves leaped into the air, then landed in a row with arms crossed, feet kicking out.

> *Brightest star of magic, fairest of the mall,*
> *There's no need to choose when you can have*
> *it all!*

Spriggans and pixies cartwheeled out of their stores carrying cashmere wraps, chiffon dresses, jackets and—

"Shoes!" Kara was so happy she could barely breathe.

Glorious shoes in every style and color, pair after pair, each more awesome than the last.

"I'll take those!" She pointed to a pair of strappy gold heels. "And that and that and that!"

Wrapped shoeboxes and shopping bags flew through the air practically burying Goldie as the d-fly tottered beneath the growing pile.

"That should last me until back to school shopping." Kara grinned in satisfaction.

Pixies chased Lyra with pink, silver, and rhinestone collars.

"I don't need a new collar, I have thirty-five already!" the cat yelled. *"Kara!"*

> *You wear the hottest brands and start the*
> *newest trends,*
> *There's always more in every store,*
> *the shopping never ends*
> *Power shopping princess,*
> *your fashion star is blazing,*
> *What we have is what you want,*
> *guaranteed—*

"Amazing!" Kara leaped and shouted. She grabbed

Lyra's front paws and danced her back and forth, caught in a frenzied fashion fever.

"*Snap out of it!*" Lyra roared. "*We have to find the unicorns!*"

"Not now, this is everything I ever wanted!"

Arms held high, Kara shimmied and swayed. The music picked up, moving faster and louder.

> *Try on these shoes they go with that vest*
> *A necklace, a bracelet, may we suggest*
> *Until you are happy we will not rest*

Beaming, Kara headed toward the shiny escalators. There were at least three levels she hadn't even seen!

"*Kara!*" Lyra pushed through a wall of gift boxes, locking her green eyes on her bonded's. "*You're under a spell.*"

"Must ... fight it ... stop ... shopping!" Goldie landed on Kara's shoulder, paws shaking Kara's neck.

All at once, Kara felt dizzy, as if she were seeing everything through a haze.

Lights and glass, steel and chrome spun around her, as the boggles, pixies, and spriggans disappeared back into their stores.

"Wow." She inhaled deeply, then looked at Lyra. "Hey! How come they all knew I was going to be here when *I* didn't know I was going to be here?"

Her eyes strayed to the glowing power crystal in her hand. How did that get there?

"There's something very strange about that jewel." Lyra swished her tail.

"I don't remember Tasha saying anything about a power-shopping crystal," Kara said slowly.

She sensed the pull of the jewel's magic, but it didn't feel like the other power crystals the mages had found.

"I wish I knew more about this power crystal," she mused.

She looked up, eyes widening. Directly across from her was a store she hadn't noticed before:

GOBLIN FELDMAN'S EMPORIUM
WHAT WE DON'T HAVE, YOU DON'T WANT

The windows glittered with dazzling objects.

"Hey, look at that." Kara grasped the power crystal and headed toward the sparkling store.

"Wait, come back!" Lyra and Goldie followed their brave leader into the most dangerous boutique of all: a jewelry store

12

"*By the gods!*" The dragon's purple eyes widened with astonishment as he stomped toward Adriane, Drake, and Fred on his two enormous feet.

He was about Drake's size, but his horse-like head was longer and more slender. His black scales glinted in the sunlight, and deep purple slashes zigzagged across his leathery wings like lightning in the night sky.

Adriane spun into fighting position, wolf stone blazing as she faced the fearsome black creature. "That's close enough!"

Dreamer snarled and Fred dove into Adriane's pocket.

Ignoring the warrior and her wolf, the dragon focused on Drake. *"It is a sign from the High Wyvern! A red crystal dragon to aid me on my quest and endure all the pain—rrr, I mean, share the glory with me.*"

"*Hi,*" Drake answered. "*I'm on a quest, too.*"

The black dragon motioned to Adriane and Dreamer, his long forked tongued snaking from his tooth-filled snout. "*And you brought snacks.*"

Drake rumbled indignantly. "*That is my mama.*"

The black dragon blinked as if puzzled, then roared with laughter. "*Brother, you must be mad with the heat.*"

"What did you do to us back there?" Adriane demanded.

"*Silence, pitiful human!*" Silver spikes along his sinewy neck reflected glints of sun as the dragon's head snaked menacingly. "*Only the great red dragon may speak to me.*"

"Fine," the warrior growled. "Drake, ask him."

"*What did you do to us?*" Drake repeated.

The beast stomped indignantly, sending dust and rocks flying. "*Can it be true? A dragon bonded with a human? Unthinkable!*"

"Think whatever you want," Adriane said. In other circumstances, meeting another dragon would've been cool. But this one was getting on her nerves. "Just answer the question: What happened?"

The dragon's giant eyes flicked toward the warrior, sizing up the girl and her magic. He snarled and addressed Drake. "*You were attacked by the most reviled enemy of our race, a shadow dragon. It uses fear as a weapon.*"

"Shadow dragon?" Adriane asked. Tasha had mentioned

Barnes & Noble Booksellers #1979
2289 Broadway
New York, NY 10024
212-362-8835

STR:1979 REG:009 TRN:7459 CSHR:Grace C

BARNES & NOBLE MEMBER   EXP: 07/31/2010

Avalon: Web of Magic Boo
  9781934876756
  (1 @ 5.95) Member Card 10% (0.60)
  (1 @ 5.35)   5.35

Subtotal   5.35
Sales Tax (8.875%)   0.47
TOTAL   **5.82**
CASH   **20.00**
CASH CHANGE   **14.18-**

MEMBER SAVINGS   0.60

Thanks for shopping at
Barnes & Noble

V101.19   12/07/2009 01:28PM

CUSTOMER COPY

will be issued for (i) purchases made by check less than 7 days prior to the date of return, (ii) when a gift receipt is presented within 60 days of purchase, (iii) textbooks returned with a receipt within 14 days of purchase, or (iv) original purchase was made through Barnes & Noble.com via PayPal. Opened music/DVDs/audio may not be returned, but can be exchanged only for the same title if defective.

<u>After 14 days or without a sales receipt</u>, returns or exchanges will not be permitted.

Magazines, newspapers, and used books are not returnable. *Product not carried by Barnes & Noble or Barnes & Noble.com will not be accepted for return.*

Policy on receipt may appear in two sections.

Return Policy

<u>With a sales receipt</u>, a full refund in the original form of payment will be issued from any Barnes & Noble store for returns of new and unread books (except textbooks) and unopened music/DVDs/audio made within (i) 14 days of purchase from a Barnes & Noble retail store (except for purchases made by check less than 7 days prior to the date of return) or (ii) 14 days of delivery date for Barnes & Noble.com purchases (except for purchases made via PayPal). A store credit for the purchase price will be issued for (i) purchases made by check less than 7 days prior to the date of return, (ii) when a gift receipt is presented within 60 days of purchase, (iii) textbooks returned with a receipt within 14 days of purchase, or (iv) original purchase was made through Barnes & Noble.com via PayPal. Opened music/DVDs/audio may not be returned, but can be exchanged only for the same title if defective.

<u>After 14 days or without a sales receipt</u>, returns or exchanges will not be permitted.

Magazines, newspapers, and used books are not returnable. *Product not carried by Barnes & Noble or Barnes & Noble.com will not be accepted for return.*

Policy on receipt may appear in two sections.

dangerous creatures being spotted all along the web. But shadow creatures! The warrior remembered fighting a horde of the ferocious magic feeders on the Spirit Trail. They would need powerful magic to survive outside the astral planes.

The dragon puffed out his chest. *"I, the greatest warrior since Dwrrlgaarowlrowl the Noxious, shall defeat this creature and return a hero!"*

"Hey." Adriane waved. "I'm over here."

The dragon snorted, releasing a lick of fire. *"I would rather die than become a slave to the humans."*

"We can arrange that," the warrior snapped, "but we need to find that shadow dragon. It has something we want."

The dragon hesitated, then gave in to curiosity. *"Speak, human."*

"The creature you're after has a powerful jewel. Do you know anything about it?"

The dragon thought for a minute. *"So that is why I could not vanquish the beast. It is being aided by your foul magic!"*

"We're not helping it!" Drake protested.

"We need to find it," Adriane told him.

"I have been tracking the shadow dragon for days. I had the beast right where he wanted me until you showed up." He loomed over Adriane, but took a step back when Dreamer snarled.

Adriane narrowed her eyes. "How come you didn't follow it?"

"*Rrrrr,*" the dragon rumbled. "*He'd be expecting that.*"

Dreamer snorted. "*You were scared, too.*"

"*Silence!*" The dragon fired a burst of flame over the mistwolf's head. "*I fear nothing!*"

"That's enough out of you." Silver fire burst from Adriane's fingers, singeing the tip of the dragon's nose.

The beast went cross-eyed as he pulled his head back sharply.

Adriane lowered her arm, letting the magic dissipate into harmless sparks. "What's your name?"

The dragon turned his back on Adriane, moving surprisingly fast for a creature so large. His long spiked tail swished across the red sand. "*I do not speak with humans,*" he huffed.

Adriane sighed. "Ask him what his name is, Drake."

"*I'm Drake. What's your name?*"

The black dragon slowly turned, head raised high in the air. "*I am the great hunter, Gwylrrtrwrx.*"

Adriane blinked at the incomprehensible grumble. "What did he say?"

Drake cocked his head. "*I think his name is Runs-with-Tail.*"

"Rrrr, it is my training name until I complete my warrior quest. I will slay the shadow dragon and then I will be given a full name."

"So, Runs, um, Gwyx, it seems we're on the same quest. You want the shadow dragon, we want the jewel," Adriane said.

"Dragon Home is counting on me. They sent me because I'm their greatest warrior."

"Do you know how to fight this creature?" Adriane did not want to be rendered helpless again by the shadow dragon's strange power.

"Of course I know!" he roared, then eyed Drake. *"Rrrr, the question is, how would* you *fight it, brother Drake?"*

Drake considered. *"He will not be as strong without the power crystal."*

"Exactly! We will take its power source and I will annihilate, eviscerate, mashed potato—!"

"Hold that thought, Megatron." Adriane leaned in close to her friends.

"In the name of the High Wyvern, I command you to help me on my quest!" the black dragon bellowed.

"Uh uh." Adriane held up a finger. Gwyx flinched.

Drake lowered his giant head as Fred hopped onto Adriane's shoulder.

Gwyx inched closer, trying to eavesdrop.

"Pffffft!" Fred shot a raspberry and the big dragon leaped back.

"What do you think, Team Wolf?" Adriane whispered.

Dreamer shifted uneasily. *"I smelled Gwyx, but I couldn't track the shadow dragon."*

"Since Gwyx can, I think we should team up," the warrior stated.

"He said this place is Dragon Home," Drake said excitedly.

The warrior smiled. "We should learn more about it."

"I don't trust him," Dreamer snarled.

"There is something strange about him," Adriane conceded.

"I don't like how he speaks to you." Drake huffed a puff of smoke.

"Every culture is different," Adriane said calmly. "For now, you're the boss."

"Right." Fred nodded.

"No, I meant Drake. We'll play along with him until we find the crystal."

"Okay, Mama."

Adriane patted Drake, then offered Gwyx a dramatic bow. "The great red dragon will address you."

"Ah, excellent."

"We will go with you," Drake announced.

"Splendid!" Gwyx beamed, then quickly scowled. *"I am accustomed to battling alone, but I cannot deny my brother if he wishes to accompany me."*

"It is an honor to aid to such a great warrior as you," Adriane gushed.

"I'll show him who he thinks we are!"

"You will tell me more about Dragon Home?" Drake asked eagerly.

Adriane grinned. None of them had met another full sized dragon before—not even Drake. Maybe her baby would learn more about his own kind.

"Brother, you have only to ask. I only pity you for taking abuse from such a... loud human."

"RoaRR!" Drake agreed angrily, then winked a big golden eye at Adriane.

The warrior stifled her giggles. "Master Drake, those hunters will be here soon. We must bustle."

Gwyx lifted his head high. *"I, the greatest warrior of Dragon Home, shall find the shadow dragon!"*

The warrior hopped into Drake's saddle. Dreamer scrambled up behind her.

Adriane gave Gwyx the most respectful look she could muster. "Lead on, O mighty hunter."

"To victory!" Gwyx trumpeted, bellowing a jet of fire into the air.

With a beat of mighty wings, the two dragons soared into the reddened skies.

13

"*I*T'S HORRIBLE!" THE kobold leader wailed, shielding his watering red eyes from the bright sunlight.

They stood in a verdant valley filled with huge flowers, babbling brooks, and trees laden with ripe fruit. Snowcapped mountains surged to the skies, protectively encircling the pristine vale. The air sparkled, warmed by the dazzling sun.

But Emily knew something was wrong. Magic sparked through her jewel, itching like sandpaper against her wrist.

The rest of the kobolds cowered, desperately seeking shade beneath fragrant peach and apricot trees. "Fix it, hurry!" they implored.

"Emily, what are they talking about?" Lorren inhaled the sweet air.

The healer studied the kobolds and frowned. Each creature adapted to its natural environment. The kobolds should be living somewhere darker and colder. "This environment is totally wrong for them," she explained. "The sun is way too bright for their large eyes, and their thick fur is too heavy for this warm climate."

"Are you sure this is your home?" Ozzie asked the kobold. "Maybe you got lost."

"We know our home when we don't see it!" the creature wailed.

"Ozzie," Emily murmured, raising her rainbow jewel. "Give me a boost."

The ferret's orange gem sparkled as he hopped to her side.

Gingerly reaching out with her magic, Emily focused on a patch of bright purple daisies, watching intently as a halo of light blossomed. Plants had magical auras too, more subtle than magical animals, but visible to Emily's heightened vision. The daisies, with their large smooth petals and strong stems, appeared perfectly healthy. But when Emily looked deeper, she saw the truth: The flowers' aura was a jumble of red and blue, like two different colored ribbons tangled together in a knot. Instinctively, Emily sensed the blue magic was the daisy's true magical aura. The red magic was eating away at it like a virus. Emily shuddered. She'd seen this before, when the water magic of Aldenmor had made the sea dragons sick.

Widening her magical vision only confirmed her fears. This strange red magic polluted the land, twisting the natural blue aura out of shape.

"Ouch." Ozzie winced, feeling the healer's shock.

Emily whispered, "This whole place hurts."

"You mean the land is sick?" Lorren asked.

Emily nodded grimly. "Yes. It isn't supposed to look like this."

Once, she had felt the pain of Ravenswood when the forest spirit was corrupted. But here the land itself hurt.

Lorren's mouth was tight with concern. "The only magic I know that could do that is a power crystal."

Emily agreed. "We need to find it before it does more damage."

"Please help us, great weaver of magic," the kobolds wailed.

"You can actually heal the land?" Lorren's eyes went wide.

"No way! This isn't like healing an animal," Ozzie exclaimed. "You can't risk something like this on your own."

Ozzie was right. This was new territory. The only way to heal this land was to reweave its magic back into its original pattern. She would have to amplify her magic through a web of animals, as she had done on Aldenmor. But her new powers had hurt so many. This could be even riskier.

But what choice did she have? The kobolds, huddled in a miserable clump, were suffering. She was a healer and these creatures needed her help. "I have to try."

"You sure about this?" Ozzie's brown eyes were wide with worry.

Know this, healer. Your power for weaving magic surpasses even hers.

The words of the Dark Sorceress echoed in her mind. Ozzie was right to be concerned.

But Emily was not the Spider Witch. And if her Level Two powers enabled her to heal in this new way, she had to take the next step.

Deep down Emily already knew she could do it.

She spread her arms wide. "Ready?"

Without waiting for Ozzie's response, the healer enveloped the clump of daisies with a wave of glowing colors. Instantly her jewel flashed dark as magic prickled along her skin. Taking a deep breath, she wrapped her power around the voracious red threads. Her fingers moved through air as she gently tugged at the red, trying to unravel it. To her surprise, it came loose easily. A loop of red magic separated from the daisies' blue auras and floated before her eyes. And she was doing this with only Ozzie's magic to support her.

"It's working!" Ozzie gasped.

The daisies began shimmering, changing. With bright sparks their purple petals melted into sharp red spikes, and the green stems twisted to woody brown.

"The bugbear pod!" the kobolds cried happily.

"I don't believe it!" Lorren said, stunned.

Emily barely heard him. Encouraged, she expanded her healing web over the lush valley floor. She tugged at the red magic, her fingers moving faster as she tore it loose, allowing the blue pattern to regain its original shape.

The mountain peaks wavered and changed, their bright colors sliding off like melting snow. Fruit trees groaned as their bark shifted back into thorny branches; the whisper of the rushing stream silenced, becoming the ominous quiet of a dense bog. Mist seeped over the craggy land like a dank cloak, chilling her to the bone.

She was vaguely aware of Ozzie, Lorren, and the kobolds gasping in awe as she wove away the red magic faster and faster. It was working. Everything was turning back to the way it was supposed to be. The original blue pattern shimmered across the valley, strong, renewed, and healthy once more.

She felt Ozzie using his magic to gently slow hers down, but Emily didn't want to stop. She dove deeper, spiraling to the very core of the land.

In a brilliant flash, she found coils of silver lacing beneath the land like pipelines—the magic web itself, feeding magic into the vale. The web's dazzling auras danced before her enhanced vision. It was the most incredible thing she'd seen yet, almost too much to take in.

A thread of the red magic caught her eye, trailing

away far into the distance. Emily's heart thudded with excitement. It was still connected to the source!

Pushing the limits of her power, Emily widened her magical vision even further, following the thread. Sure enough, it led to a gleaming power crystal, floating like a sparkling vision on the magic web.

She pushed forward, but the closer she got, the farther away the crystal seemed to go, just out of reach, as if something were constantly pulling it from her grasp. With a mighty effort, Emily flung her magic toward the crystal—and came to a screeching halt.

The kobold's section of web abruptly ended, trailing off into an immense black chasm.

She gasped at this startling discovery. The kobolds' home was not connected to the rest of the web!

She could not follow the power crystal without creating some kind of bridge to link the two sections of web. The power crystal must have isolated the kobolds' home. Why else would this land be completely cut off? She was going to need more than Ozzie's magical back-up to weave the two sections of web together.

Instinctively, Emily summoned more magic, reaching out to any animal that could hear her.

Power rushed through her, swift and sharp, as animal strength amplified her magic. But this magic looked nothing like the bright auras of the Ravenswood animals. It was dark, shadowy, reaching out for her with predatory hunger. She didn't have time to be afraid as her web blossomed into a giant network. Auras blinked so fast she couldn't tell exactly who had answered her call, only that enough of them had.

Her vision rocketed across the silvery magic web. She didn't think about how to weave this magic. She just did, her Level Two powers filling her with confidence. She was actually healing the web, her fears melting away as bright magic flew from her fingers.

Weaving the animals' magic into a bright thread, she looped it through the two edges of the severed web. In a few moments the kobolds' home was attached to the rest of the magic web. With a final tug, she pulled tight, knotting the sections of web together.

Suddenly bright spikes of magic flared across the web like a tidal wave.

Beneath her feet, the land rippled with a powerful earthquake.

Her eyes flew open. The beautiful trees and flowers had completely disappeared, revealing an ugly, dank land. Craggy volcanic mountains belched foul smoke into the gray skies. Icy rain drizzled onto thorny trees with wicked orange spikes and shriveled fruit.

The kobolds danced with joy. "Great witch, you have performed a miracle!"

Lorren regarded Emily with complete awe. "How did you do this?"

"I just could," she whispered hoarsely.

"Emily!" Tweek's voice suddenly exploded in her ear.

Fiona was sitting on her shoulder.

"Something's happened!" Tweek's voice blared from the d-fly. "The web is in total chaos!"

But Emily was too busy looking at this rewoven landscape. Dark monoliths loomed above her, glistening like black ice. Something about this place was strangely familiar.

"Where are we?" she asked.

"Our home." The kobolds grinned. "The Otherworlds!"

"We have a situation!" Tweek shouted. "Hello, is this thing on?"

Lorren shook his head. "The Otherworlds aren't even connected to the web, we couldn't possibly be there."

Ice ran through Emily's veins. The Otherworlds! That's where she had seen this place before, in terrible nightmares sent by the Dark Sorceress. It was a prison to unimaginably dark creatures. And she had just connected this awful place to the rest of the magic web!

Little Fiona hopped from foot to foot as Tweek screamed. "The Spider Witch's web just expanded! And you're right in the middle of it!"

Emily's stomach knotted with fear. What had she done? Frantically she tried to find the power crystal again. Maybe its magic would help her fix this terrible mistake.

Red lightning spiked through her jewel with a jolt. That was no power crystal. A mass of creatures, fierce and greedy, had latched onto her magic. And they knew exactly where she was.

"We have to get out of here," she said through clenched teeth.

"The Spider Witch wanted the Otherworlds attached to her web." Lorren stared at the healer.

A bloodcurdling yowl pierced the air.

"What was that?" Ozzie asked, hair frizzed on end.

"Now." Emily gasped as more and more dark creatures attached themselves to her magic.

Sleek bodies with yellow eyes moved like ghosts through the mist.

The glint of cold steel flashed as Lorren unsheathed his sword.

"Shadow cats!" The kobolds turned tail and fled, vanishing into murky caves along the mountain walls. "Hurry, take shelter with us!"

Another unearthly shriek rang out, and then another, and another.

Lorren turned toward Emily, his face pale. "We need a portal."

Saber tooth fangs and spiked tails wavered in and out of sight. As suddenly as they appeared, they vanished, leaving only glinting snarls like nightmarish Cheshire cats.

Ozzie scrambled onto Emily's shoulder and throttled little Fiona. "Find us a portal!"

Emily reeled as the shadow creatures swirled around her, ripping away shreds of her bright aura.

Lorren was at her side. "Can you run?"

"I ... think so." She tired to push wet curls from her face but she was so weak.

"Lean on me." The goblin prince draped her arm over his shoulders.

"Twigman!" Ozzie shouted.

"There are several portals directly south. They're moving fast so—"

"Run!"

Emily and Loren bolted, Ozzie falling headfirst into her backpack.

The goblin prince guided Emily quickly through the moor, veering right and left along a trail only he could make out.

She glanced over her shoulder, heart skipping a beat as she saw dozens of black smudges in the mist. They seemed to be everywhere and nowhere all at once.

"Which way?" Lorren yelled.

"Left!" They heard Tweek scream as Fiona swooped overhead, jeweled eyes whirling in distress. "Right!"

Emily dodged under a spiky tree, staggering back as a sharp thorn ripped her denim jacket.

Yellow eyes and glowing fangs leaped straight at them.

"Ahhh!" Ozzie poked his head from the pack.

Lorren's sword sliced through thin air as the swift beast soared overhead and vanished.

"Straight ahead!" Tweek guided frantically. "Wait, bear right, right!"

Slipping on the slick rocky ground, Emily and Lorren sprinted, barely thinking as they leaped over a muddy stream. She landed shin deep in slimy water, losing precious seconds as she slogged forward, breathing hard.

"Well?" Ozzie grabbed the red dragonfly.

"I'm triangulating," Tweek advised.

"I'm gonna triangle all over your head!" Ozzie yelled, squashing Fiona into the pack.

"There it is!" Lorren pointed to a glowing blue doorway drifting along a foggy ravine.

"The portal's moving," Tweek cried. "Hurry!"

"Go!" Lorren pushed Emily forward as he turned to fend off their pursuers.

Emily struggled through tangled growth, desperately fighting off the crushing attacks. Blackness swirled around her in suffocating waves as her magic was torn away.

"ROARRRRRaRR!" A deafening bellow boomed through the air, sucking the breath from Emily's lungs.

The shadow cats vanished like smoke.

"What was that?" Lorren asked incredulously.

Ozzie stood atop a small boulder, ferret stone glowing. "I call it my mantichorus."

"Nice," the goblin prince grinned.

Emily skidded to a halt at the edge of the ravine, sending rocks disappearing into deep fog below. The glittering doorway hung in the air a few feet away from the cliff's edge.

"Ozzie, come on," Emily called.

Ozzie turned his liquid brown eyes to hers. "They won't be fooled for long."

"Jump!" Lorren ordered.

The portal was too far away. Desperately, she tried to pull it closer, but her magic was ragged, weakened to the point of exhaustion. She reached out and her footing gave way. Grasping at something, anything to stop her fall, she tumbled down the ravine and crashed in a painful heap at the bottom.

"Emily!" Ozzie yelled.

Through thick mist she watched in horror as dozens of shadow cats sprang at the ferret and the prince. Heart pounding, Emily struggled to her knees, ignoring the agony in her left ankle. Hundreds of yellow eyes swarmed into the gully. She felt their cold breath run down her back, their sharp teeth hungry for her magic.

"Help!" she screamed.

A sudden explosion of light blinded her as another portal opened. She tried to shield her eyes against the purple blur that leaped from the swirling brightness. Light and sound rushed past her as she fell through the magical doorway, twisting and tumbling, reaching for her friends.

But they were no longer there.

14

"*F*ANTASTIC!"

The Dark Sorceress gazed into the seeing pool, smiling in satisfaction. On the glowing surface, the image of a blonde girl, a leopard cat, and a golden fairy dragon shimmered. The sorceress's eyes sparked greedily at the sight of the luminous crystal in the young mage's hands. Abruptly the image went blank.

She glanced at Gardener, slumped across the marble floor beside her. Shivers racked his ragged frame as the shadow creature on his back pulsed ominously.

"Aww, tired already?" the Dark Sorceress mocked.

But the magical charge had been enough to show her what she needed.

"The blazing star has found the perfect power crystal,"

she gloated. "And she snatched it right from the Spider Witch's web. I could not have planned it better myself."

"She should not have to be sacrificed." Gardener pushed lank hair from his face as he struggled to sit up.

"Don't think of it as a sacrifice. The blazing star will become a valuable ally."

"She will become a monster." Gardener's eyes flashed. "Like you."

"I am what I'm supposed to be," she shot back. "Living proof that the prophecy always comes true."

"You poisoned Aldenmor," he said angrily. "Was that part of your prophecy?"

"If I hadn't released Black Fire, the mages wouldn't even have a prophecy to test," she retorted. "The fact is, evil defines goodness."

"Choices define good and evil. We *were* the ones, Miranda, until you betrayed us. I will never forget what you did." Gardener's eyes glistened with emotion. "I would have given anything to have a bond like that."

The sorceress ignored the emptiness welling in her chest. "I am way past caring for the creature. Whatever happened that day has kept us *all* alive."

"Alive," Henry scoffed. "Silvan is half spider, whatever you are isn't close to human, and Lucinda…."

The Dark Sorceress watched the pain gleaming in his eyes. "There is always a price to pay."

"The price is too great, Miranda." Gardener shook his head. "We have lived beyond our time."

"Henry, you are right." She turned away, silver-streaked hair hiding the fierce hunger in her eyes. "I'm tired of hunting scraps of magic here and there just so I can survive. I must move on."

"The mages will stop you."

The sorceress wheeled to face him, eyes burning like fire. "I've helped these mages. I gave the warrior a power crystal, I taught the healer about her magic, and I have watched the blazing star from the beginning. Where were you? You left them without a mentor."

"They turned out all right."

The scrying pool sparked, reflecting an image of the blazing star.

"We'll see, won't we."

"I will never give you what you want."

"Oh, I think you will." The sorceress raised a clawed hand.

At once the door to the scrying chamber slid open. Rusted wheels creaked eerily in the stone room as two lizard guards entered, pushing a steel and glass cage. Murky smoke hid the roiling dark masses within.

One of the guards slid back the hatch and stepped quickly away. Mist exploded from the tank as the voracious creatures leaped free. Black as night, monstrous leeches sank long needles into Gardener's legs, arms, and torso, binding him in a nightmare of pain.

"You *will* tell me everything—and more."

15

KARA GAPED AT the brilliant display cases in the jewelry shop. Necklaces, earrings, bracelets, rings, pendants, and tiaras twinkled with glittering gems of every color, shape, and size imaginable.

"Ahhh, a potential customer."

A short, stubby, green creature stepped around the counter, his shifty eyes twinkling, wide mouth grinning from ear to ear. And what ears! Big, green, and pointed, they protruded from the sides of his wide head like wings.

"I am Goblin Feldman." He bowed, his bulbous nose nearly touching his big green feet. "I cater to only the highest level of customer. And you're pretty tall."

Kara studied the short green creature warily. "You don't look like a goblin."

"You know goblins, then?" His eyes darted around the shop suspiciously.

"Only Prince Lorren and the whole royal family," Kara boasted.

"Oh, well, *I'm* the handsome type." Feldman straightened his leather vest and white shirt. "Not like your boyfriend."

"He's not exactly my, oh never mind. I need some info on a rare gem."

Feldman's hand swept over a display case. "May I suggest an emerald collar for your feline friend and a petite peridot pendant for your fairy dragon?"

Goldie flapped her wings excitedly.

"No." Kara bent low and whispered. "A *rare* gem, magic rare."

The goblin's eyes lit up. "Ahh, wink, wink. I got what you need."

He ushered her to a case draped in red velvet. With a dramatic flair, he swept the covering aside.

Kara's jaw dropped.

"The unicorn jewel of the blazing star!" Feldman proclaimed proudly.

"Not bad." Lyra assessed the fake gem as Kara calmed the indignant Goldie with a scratch between the wings.

The jewel was slightly smaller than Kara's and the swirling colors emanated from what looked like battery-operated lights inside.

"Unique, one of a kind, absolutely guaranteed to be

authentic. It belonged to the fairy princess herself," the goblin confidently assured her.

"Gee, I guess mine must be an imitation, then." Kara casually pulled her unicorn jewel from the folds of her jacket. Twinkles of magic dazzled along the flawless pink, red, and white facets

Feldman's eyes practically popped out of his head.

"BlarPH!" Goldie blarphed.

"'Scuse me, d-fly call." Kara turned away from the amazed shopkeeper.

"Base to Star One," Tweek yelled. "Come in."

"Star One here."

"Thank goodness I finally found you. We've got some major shifts along the web and Emily—holy twig!" Tweek sputtered. "You're right on top of a power crystal!"

"Really?" Kara pulled the magnificent power crystal from her pocket. Magic danced around the room in bright sparkles.

"Where are you, exactly?" Tweek asked.

"We got sidetracked. Is everything okay with Emily?"

"Beebeebeebeep," Goldie vibrated, letting Kara know another voice was joining their magical conference call.

"Wolf Fire to Star One," Adriane sounded anxious. "I can't reach Emily. Kara, where are you?"

"Well, I'm at this mall check—"

"The mall?" Adriane asked incredulously.

"Actually, I'm in a jewelry store—"

"What!?"

"You should see this dress I found!"

"What are you talking about?" the warrior demanded, annoyed.

"Duh, only the most important school event of the year."

"You have the power crystal in your possession?" Tweek asked.

"You found a power crystal?" Adriane echoed.

"Yeah, but it's really acting weird."

"What's weird is you not doing what you're supposed to!"

"I don't even know how she got to where she is," Tweek fretted.

"Jeez, cut me some slack here." Kara was getting ticked now. Once again, every time she tried to do something on her own, everyone came down on her like she was the Dark Sorceress.

"Take the power crystal to The Garden right away!" Adriane ordered.

Kara flushed with anger. "What, you don't trust me with a crystal, is that it?"

"And don't do anything stupid."

"I wish all of you would just leave me alone!" Kara yelled.

"Your mage-nificence!" the goblin store owner shouted. He had he overheard every word of Kara's conversation. "The blazing star no less! On a quest to save the web and—is that a real power crystal of Avalon?"

"Realer than your unicorn jewels," Kara snapped.

"Bah, that's for tourists," he scoffed.

Kara rolled her eyes. "Star One to Base." She tapped Goldie's head but all she heard was a tiny tummy grumble. "I can't believe they all hung up on me!"

The little d-fly just shrugged.

Lyra nudged Kara. *"Adriane's right. We have to head back."*

"We will, but you have to admit this jewel is pretty flooie."

"We said we would take the power crystal to The Garden," Lyra reminded her.

Goldie nodded at Kara.

"What's if it's tainted like the one that turned Marina?" Kara asked them.

Goldie nodded at Lyra.

"Besides, we don't even know how we got here." Kara studied the power crystal. So dazzling and bright and beautiful. How could it possibly be tainted?

"What can you tell us about this?" Kara handed the crystal to Feldman.

Feldman plucked a jeweler's loop from his vest pocket and squinted hard to hold the lens in place. He peered at her with his magnified, blinking eyeball. "No one knows more about magic jewels than me. Except maybe my cousin Maury, but he's retired."

He held the dazzling jewel as close to the lens as he could, then at arms length. Not satisfied, the goblin smelled it, bit it between his big yellow teeth and bonked it with his knobby knuckles.

"So what kind of power crystal is it?" Kara asked impatiently.

"Well, you got your orbs, talismans, crystal balls," Feldman pointed to various objects on display. "You got your evil eyes, you got your hexed spheres, bonding crystals, data storage crystals—"

"And?"

"What you got isn't any of those."

"Ah ha!" Kara exclaimed. "Um, so what is it?"

The lens popped out of Feldman's eye as he turned his attention to his three guests. "How did you say you got here?"

"We were on the web being attacked by huge spiders, and then suddenly we were here," Kara explained.

"Did you happen to *wish* you were here?"

"I didn't even know this place existed." Kara thought for a minute. "Now that you mention it, I did wish to be in the most wonderful place ever."

"I see." He returned to the crystal. "Hmm, let's try something. Are you guys hungry from all your mage adventures?"

"Yeah," Kara answered. "I wish I had a milkshake."

SpRoing!

"Yeow!" Feldman leaped back as a tall glass filled with frothy liquid appeared on the counter.

"What is that?"

The goblin prodded the dark substance spilling over the brim with a stubby finger and tasted. "Chocolate shake, creamy too."

"Oh, thank you," Kara took a sip from the straw then passed it to Goldie.

"You're welcome, but I didn't do it, you did," the goblin shopkeeper told them.

"I did?"

"What you've got here is a wishing crystal," he declared.

"I've never heard of a wishing crystal." Lyra eyed the milkshake suspiciously.

"Wish for something else," Feldman suggested, handing the crystal back.

Kara considered. "I wish for a hot dog for Goldie and a hamburger for Lyra."

Pop! Splat!

A tray of cocktail wieners materialized, followed by a platter of thick juicy burgers. A huge basket of steaming crispy fries popped up beside them, complete with organic ketchup.

"No way!" Kara raised the crystal in awe. "That's exactly how they serve it at Rocket Burgers!"

Goldie happily nibbled on the pint-sized hot dogs while Lyra nosed the burgers warily.

"Yup, you have one genuine wishing crystal," Feldman confirmed. "Very rare, imbued with strong magic, elemental in nature. It transforms thought and materializes—"

"I wish it would rain popcorn!"

Kapow!

Vats of popcorn exploded all over the shop, covering everything in fragrant fluffy piles.

"This rocks!" Kara cried, holding the unicorn power crystal high above her head. "I wish for an iPod and a new stereo, a wide screen laptop, a Wii—"

Dozens of boxes rained down on Kara.

"Stop, stop, stop!" Feldman cried. "Do you want to turn into an ogre?"

"No, but could I turn someone *else* into an ogre?"

"Yeowow!" Feldman's scream echoed across the store as a bright pink Corvette convertible appeared in a puff of smoke, knocking over several display cases and pushing the goblin out the back door.

"You don't even have a license." Lyra peered into the front seat, Goldie perched on her head.

"Woohoo!" Kara danced around the gleaming car.

"Be careful with that crystal," Lyra warned.

"Geez, why does everyone freak out whenever I use magic?" Kara's eyes opened wide. "Wait! I know exactly what I want." She raised the crystal high and commanded, "I wish I had another power crystal!"

Nothing happened. She held the power crystal tighter, willing her magic though it.

"I so *totally* wish I had another power crystal." She looked around for something big and sparkly. Still nothing. "It's broken!" she wailed.

"What?" Feldman shouted, wading his way through boxes, bags, and popcorn.

"I want another power crystal," Kara demanded.

"You want two?"

"Long story," Kara replied.

"She broke one," Goldie explained.

"Okay, short story, but this crystal still won't grant my wish." Eyes shut, Kara wished and wished again.

"No, no, no!" Feldman waved his hands in the air. "It can't make another power crystal because that would use up all its magic, and if you keep wishing you're going to drain it, too."

"Well, how do I get another one?"

"You know anything about alchemy?" the goblin asked.

"No."

"Me either. I mean, making a power crystal ain't like popping corn, girl. You've got to have a proper crystal storage device crafted from the strongest minerals, then enchanted with great magic."

"Yeah, yeah, yeah," Kara said impatiently. "Where do I get that stuff?"

"I run an honest business, but occasionally I have customers who want, how shall I put this, more exotic items." Feldman rubbed his hands together nervously. "But I must respect their privacy. There's no way I can reveal the name of a valued client."

Kara held the unicorn power crystal high. "Maybe I'll just wish the entire web knew about your little unicorn jewel scam."

"Logan," Feldman said immediately. "He's the most nefarious, notorious, nebulous purveyor of the dark arts."

"Dark arts?" Lyra asked worriedly. *"That doesn't sound good."*

"Logan is one of my best customers. Tell him he owes me, let's see …" Feldman whipped an account book from his vest pocket. "Five million starstones."

"Why don't you tell him yourself?" Kara challenged.

"I'd go, but I hate any slight inconveniences—like death." The goblin gulped.

The blazing star grinned at Lyra, her eyes shining with determination. "Lyra, we have to see this guy! Tasha's got no leads on how to replace that crystal."

Lyra growled, not liking it.

"Please, please, please." She gave her friend her most irresistible wide-eyed look.

"But then we find our way back to The Garden."

Kara eyed Feldman. "Okay, so what creepy, awful place do we have to go to find this Logan dude?"

"He hangs at a club called The Black Rose." Feldman pointed. "Take the escalator down and make a left."

Kara blinked. "All righty, then."

Feldman hopped into the pink Corvette and waved good-bye. "Keep it real."

16

"WHAT THE—!" Ozzie looked one way, then hopped around and looked the other.

There were no signs of the shadow cats. No blazing, yellow eyes, no sharp, chomping teeth. But there was something else just as terrifying. Heading straight towards him were Tiffany, Molly, and Heather leading twenty tourists through the Ravenswood Preserve.

"This is a famous garden," Tiffany called out, reading from her notes.

"We can see that," a grouchy old lady grumbled.

"These heirloom roses were planted in 1836," Heather added.

"Impressive," the lady commented. "They look brand new."

"My feet hurt," complained a little kid.

"Where's all the animals?" his mother demanded.

"Ozzie, over here," a voice whispered.

"Gah!" Ozzie spun around.

Lorren was hiding behind a hedge wall several meters away.

In a single bound, the ferret dove into the nearest bush.

"Where's Emily?" the bush asked, eyes shifting warily.

"I don't know," Lorren answered. "Where are *we*?"

"That piece of shrubbery popped us back to Ravenswood!"

"Nice place," Lorren observed.

"I'm gonna wring that dOoi gAf—!"

"Someone's coming." Lorren pointed to the group advancing toward them. "Quiet."

The ferret stone erupted with static.

"GaH!"

"Base to Fuzzy One," Tweek shouted. "There's been a major shift in the web!"

"Where's Emily?" Ozzie whispered harshly.

"I lost her signal, but yours is loud and clear. Where are you?" Tweek's voice became highly agitated. "O me twig, you could be anywhere!"

Ozzie poked his head from the bush and glared up at the library windows gleaming over the backyard of the estate.

"Go to the window," Ozzie instructed calmly.

"What?"

"The window." Ozzie waved to the tiny bundle of twigs peering outside. "We're right here, you twig!"

"Inconceivable!" Sticks and moss plastered themselves against the pane in surprise.

"Get us back to Emily!" Ozzie shook his paw. "You, you, you—"

"Portals are opening all over the place," Tweek squeaked. "Power crystals, web flux, wild magic—I can't keep track!"

"Lorren!"

Ozzie jumped as a concerned green face popped into the bushes beside them.

"Tash!" Lorren hugged his goblin friend. "We got separated from Emily and somehow ended up here. What are you doing?"

"Making sure the tour doesn't wander through a random portal," Tasha said as several duck-waddling quiffles squashed in beside them. "Something's happened."

"I'll say," Tweek confirmed. "I had to completely reconfigure my web map to match the new pattern."

"Can you locate Emily's jewel?" Lorren asked Tasha.

"It's very faint." Tasha's hand-held jewel locator blinked with light. "But it's definitely on the web."

"Can you guide us there?"

"There a portal moving through the forest behind the sculpture gardens." Tasha pointed. "If you hurry, you could—"

"Let's go!" Ozzie dashed from the bushes.

"Oooh, there's that cute little ferret," a voice cried out.

"Doh!" Ozzie stopped short, trapped as tourists swarmed around him. Three quiffles came barreling into his rear.

"SplaaPh."

"Hey, we don't have notes on those animals," Heather said.

Molly beamed. "Those are rare ducks from . . . France."

"Ooooh, a French duck!" Cameras clicked as the quiffles posed and preened their head-feathers.

"Do a trick, Ozzie," a lady called out, recognizing the ferret from the Ravenswood brochure.

"No way—oop!" Ozzie slapped his paws over his mouth.

"Did he just talk?" Tiffany whispered.

Ozzie shook his head.

Heather bent over the wide-eyed, frozen ferret. "What's with you, ferret?"

"All part of the show," Lorren stepped from the hedges.

"Who's that?" Tiffany and Heather exchanged a look while Molly checked Kara's carefully scripted notes.

"Greetings from the Fairy Realms, good people." Lorren bowed with a flourish. "I am Prince Lorren."

The tour group clapped energetically. "What a show!"

"And such marvelous makeup."

"This is truly a magical place," a delighted woman declared.

"He must be the gardener, he's got a green thumb," someone cracked.

"Go ahead, Ozzie." Lorren smiled.

"Huh?"

"Do your trick."

Ozzie shuffled his feet, moving forward and back, then cart wheeled across the grass.

The group cheered enthusiastically while Tasha and the quiffles sent a herd of deer and peacocks into the crowd. The tourists turned their cameras as the animals strolled among them in search of treats.

Ozzie moonwalked behind a rose bush and vanished.

Molly, Tiffany, and Heather looked confused as the group happily fed the animals.

Ozzie ran as fast as his little legs could move toward the portal, Lorren, Tasha, and the quiffles hot on his heels.

Tasha waved her jewel locator at Lorren. "The Spider Witch's web has expanded!"

Ozzie skidded to a halt at the forest's edge. Bright magic crackled between the tall firs.

"Heads up," he said, aiming a beam of orange ferret power at the wandering portal. As the magic hit, planes of light converged into a whirling doorway.

"Emily attached the Otherworlds to the Spider Witch's web." Lorren looked at Tasha grimly. "I was just about to tell you."

"What? Why would she do that?" Tasha demanded.

"We don't know exactly what happened!" Ozzie defended the healer. "We have to find her."

"Look." Tasha held her blinking device in Ozzie's face. The golden dot indicating Ravenswood was surrounded by green tendrils of the witch's web. "The Spider Witch has got Ravenswood surrounded."

"We know what to do," Rasha, the quiffle, said determinedly. "The warrior taught us how to work with Stormbringer. We will protect Ravenswood."

"That portal will only stay open for two more minutes, hurry!" Tweek cut in.

"Where will this take us?" Lorren asked, facing the swirling doorway.

"Directly to Emily's jewel," the E.F. rattled. "Or you could fall into a black abyss of nothingness from which you will never return."

"You first," Ozzie said to Lorren.

"Hurry!" Tasha cried.

The crackling portal warped and began to drift away.

Lorren and Ozzie looked at each other. Each knew time was critical. Emily was in real trouble.

"Keep it together, twig guy!" Ozzie screamed as he soared head first into the portal.

"Look out! Portal flux—pO.Ot!"

The last thing Ozzie heard was an explosion of twigs flying all over the library.

17

"*T*HAT ADRIANE HAS some nerve hanging up on me!" In spite of all the fun she'd had in the Fashion Realm, Kara was hurt by Adrianne's diss. She juggled dozens of shopping bags as she descended the escalator, in search of the mysterious Logan.

"She didn't hang up, you wished her away," Lyra pointed out.

"Oh." Kara squeezed her eyes shut. "I unwish not to talk to my friends."

Nothing happened.

Kara arched an eyebrow at Goldie.

The golden dragonfly shrugged. "Line's dead."

"Like I need Bruin Hilda's help anyway," Kara scoffed.

"You can't do this alone," Lyra reminded her gently.

"You're right. Here, carry these." Kara slung an armload of dress bags over Lyra's back.

"All this shopping has gone to your head," Lyra grumbled.

Kara smacked her forehead. "You're so right! I wish all this stuff would go to my bedroom!"

Her mountain of packages vanished in a twinkle of magic.

"See, I'm fine. I don't need anything else." Kara wandered off the escalator, which led into another bank of shops. "Except maybe this lamp."

"Ooooo," Goldie whistled.

"And that chair."

"Focus!" Lyra nosed Kara onto the escalator leading to the basement.

There were no bright storefronts or food stalls here. Only a long, empty hallway. The thud of a throbbing bass resonated through the floor, hinting at very cool sounds coming from the end of the dark passage.

"Walk this way," directed Kara.

Lyra and Goldie sauntered down the dim hallway following in their bonded's footsteps.

Turning a corner, the blazing star stopped short. Red velvet ropes led to a set of steel doors emblazoned with the insignia of a Black Rose. Two massive stone ogres stood on either side. A trendy club! Excellent! Kara eagerly reached out to open the door.

"ID," a deep voice boomed.

The statues were glaring at her—they were alive!

"Um, we're looking for Logan," she said sweetly. "I was told he could help me with magic tech support."

Stone eyes glowed. Abruptly the steel doors swung open and the hulking guards stepped aside.

"I got game." Kara winked at Lyra.

Pounding percussion and heavy bass enveloped them as they entered the dark club. On a raised platform near the wide dance floor, a wiry spriggan DJ hipped and hopped, scratching away on twin turntables. Against the walls were a few dozen booths illuminated by solitary blue candles. The place seemed almost empty, but Kara saw Lyra's eyes narrow as the cat spotted movement in a crimson velvet booth. Two more stone figures guarded whoever sat in the shadows.

"Guys, is this cool or what?" Kara yelled over the music as she moved past a long table edged with neon light. Several fancily dressed goblins and mysterious fairy creatures turned to watch her pass.

"Word up." Goldie sat on Kara's shoulder, grooving to the beat.

Kara took a deep breath as she approached the plush booth. Logan was probably some ancient old wizard. She'd need all her skills of diplomacy to handle this geezer.

"Whazzzafuzz!" A green creature with horns and a long tail suddenly leaped from the table, cackling wildly.

The size of a small monkey, it ran around Lyra shooting sparks from its nose. "Who let the cat out? Who? Who? Who? Who?"

Lyra growled deep in her throat, ready to swat the bizarre pest.

"Are you Logan?" Kara asked incredulously.

Laughter spilled from the darkened booth. "Dimwiddie, don't be rude."

"Magic time!" The green creature ran back to its master.

"I am Logan," the silky voice continued.

Kara peered into the shadows. She could make out a pair of pale hands illuminated by flickering light. Black polish gleamed on the nails of long white fingers. As her eyes adjusted to the darkness, she noticed several ornate rings that caught the light. Some kind of tribal tattoo snaked from the back of his wrist under a silky white shirt and black velvet jacket.

"Hello. I'm Kara Davies," she said with a bright smile.

Piercing black eyes raked over Lyra, then widened as he saw Goldie perched beneath Kara's golden tresses.

"How much for the fairy dragon?"

"What?" Kara blurted, taken aback.

"The fairy dragon. How much?"

Kara's unicorn jewel flashed an angry red. "She's not for sale and don't you touch a scale on her head!" Kara scanned the guards, suddenly unsure of what she had walked into.

"My mistake." Pale hands raised in defense.

A moment of silence followed as he scrutinized her.

"Remarkable. I've never seen one bond with anybody. But then again, you're not just anybody, you're the blazing star."

"I guess my rep precedes me," Kara boasted nervously.

Logan chuckled. "Yes. You were quite the sensation in the mall."

The blazing star was suddenly self-conscious. She barely stopped to wonder how he knew about her musical welcome.

"You always travel without a chaperone?"

"Do I need one?" Kara asked.

Black eyes turned to Lyra. The cat's lips pulled back in a snarl, revealing razor teeth. The answer was clear.

"Point taken."Again, he chuckled, warm and friendly. There was no hint of a threat.

"Goblin Feldman said you could help me."

"Helping isn't exactly what I'm known for."

"Maybe it's time to change your image," Kara suggested smoothly.

"Oh? What's wrong with it?" He leaned forward into the light.

It took all her blazing star power to remain cool. This was no old, wizened crony. The flickering lights illuminated a teenage face, only a few years older than she was. His longish blonde hair was streaked with three shades of pale highlights, setting off his dark eyes and handsome, angular face. In his streamlined black velvet blazer and slick designer jeans, Logan looked more like a rock star than a user of dark magic.

Noting Kara's appraisal, a slow smile spread across his curvy lips. Logan knew exactly how hot he was and he wasn't afraid to show it.

Kara recovered her poise quickly. "Point taken."

"Dimwiddie, get our guests some ice tea," Logan ordered.

"Blazzzah! Get it yourself."

Logan gave the creature an exasperated look and it skittered away across the room.

"Gremlins." He shrugged. "Please, sit."

Kara perched on the edge of the cushioned booth, Lyra standing protectively close. Goldie hopped onto the table, helping herself to peanuts.

"Nice place," Kara said, scanning the chic club.

"Bit noisy." With a wave of his hand, the music lowered to a soft pulse. "The three mages are quite famous—the 'it' girls of the web, you could say. But none as famous as the blazing star."

She didn't know quite how to react—she wanted to remain steady, cool, focused. She *so* could not. "You're not what I expected," she blurted.

"Nor are you," he countered.

Kara couldn't help staring at his winning smile. Logan was gorgeous.

"Let me guess …" Logan shifted closer, making her heart beat like a drum.

"Level One blazing star, using a jewel of the unicorns, bonded with this magnificent cat—"

"Level Two, actually," Kara corrected him.

Logan's look of admiration melted her. "So you have a paladin protector."

"Fire stallion." Kara smiled proudly.

"Fire, of course." He leaned forward, genuinely interested. "Impressive."

"What kind of mage are you?" she asked, becoming more comfortable. "I mean, Feldman made you out to be like this total dark magic wiz."

"I'm not strictly a mage." Logan smiled again. "I am fairy."

"A fairy?" Kara was astonished. She peered into the shadows, searching for a pair of glittering wings.

Logan followed Kara's gaze, then grinned at Lyra. "Not every creature reveals its magic right away. Besides, wings can be awfully uncomfortable, don't you agree?"

Lyra pinned the dark fairy in her green gaze, unimpressed.

Kara flashed on the last fairy creature that had charmed her. That creature had turned out to be shape-shifting monster. She turned a hard look toward Logan.

"If you're a Skultum, you better tell me *right* now," she whispered threateningly.

"Skultum?" Logan laughed and brushed his hair back, revealing a pair of pointy ears. "If you faced a Skultum, you are indeed a force to be reckoned with."

Kara smiled back. "Totally."

"No, I am most certainly not a Skultum," he said sincerely. "Although some call my magic dark, but you know how people love to talk."

"Tell me about it." Kara nodded as if she knew exactly what he was talking about.

"I study all kinds of magic, mage, goblin, fairy, warlock. You bond with animals. I have found it useful to bond with… a rarer breed of creature."

"May the horse be with you!" the little gremlin yelled, tottering across the dance floor balancing a tray of drinks.

"Um, yeah," Kara agreed. "Right on."

"So how goes the great mage quest?" Logan asked, taking a glass of iced tea.

"Great." Kara beamed, and then frowned. Geez, did the entire universe know what the mages were doing? Well, so much for playing games. She needed his help. "We're searching for nine power crystals."

"The keys to Avalon."

"Yes." She felt Lyra nudge her side. Be careful.

Kara shrugged off the warning. "'Cept, I…lost one of the crystals."

He nodded, waiting for her to continue.

"And Feldman said you could help me make another one."

"Ah, that's why you're here."

"And I just found this one." She took out the large

unicorn shaped crystal, suddenly eager to impress this hottie. The power crystal spilled jewel light across the glass table. "But it's acting really weird."

"May I?"

Kara placed the crystal in his hands.

"This isn't the original shape." Logan studied the crystal carefully. "Looks like it copied your unicorn jewel when it bonded to you."

"It's a wishing crystal," she told him.

"Fascinating. So it gave you what you wanted."

"The catch is I can't undo my wish."

"A wish is only as strong as the emotion behind it," Logan explained.

Kara thought for a moment. "I guess I was pretty mad when I wished not to talk to my friends."

"Mage magic is based on emotions. That's what makes it so unpredictable." A slow grin spread across his face. "I'll bet you've lost your magic more than once, or thought you did."

Kara was startled by his insight. She, Emily, and Adriane had all "lost" their magic before.

"I thought so. Mage magic is powerful but highly unstable. Anger, self doubt, jealousy, fear, greed. You get the picture. The stronger the emotions, the harder it is to control the magic."

Kara listened to every word. This was the first time anyone had ever explained why she had such trouble controlling her magic. It had gone flooie more times than she cared to remember. Each time she'd been on a roller coaster of emotions. What Logan said made perfect sense.

Kara tossed her hair over her shoulder. "So what's your magic?"

"I study the arcane arts. Precise magic based on teachings handed down for centuries. I add my own special touch, of course, but there's no emotion involved. Arcane magic is an exact science. A craft, if you will."

Kara looked puzzled.

"Didn't your mentors tell you about the arcane arts?"

"Never had one."

That got another chuckle. "You really are quite amazing."

"True." Kara gave him a dazzling smile.

Even though her instincts told her to be wary of this too-cute-to-be-true fairy, she liked him. She knew she shouldn't, but she did. Kara prided herself on her people radar, and something about him was genuine, even if his persona was silky smooth Armani.

"So, can these scientific arts help me make another power crystal?" Kara asked hopefully.

"I doubt it."

Kara stared at him, shocked.

"If you don't help me, the Spider Witch and the Dark Sorceress will take over the entire magic web!" she exclaimed.

"Wake me when the party starts," Logan yawned.

Kara was taken aback by his indifference. "Don't you care?"

"Why should I care what shape the web takes or who controls it? It's all good for business."

Kara's jaw clenched. "And what kind of *business* might that be?"

"I supply exotic goods to my customers. Shadow silk, rune cloth, soul dust, dragonscales, signets, stuff like that. These days everyone wants magic jewels. We're such slaves to fashion, don't you think?"

"For sure. But you're the only one who can help me. I just *have* to make another power crystal. I'm the blazing star and I have to prove I'm better than—"

What was she saying? This was about saving Avalon and the magic web, not about who was the most powerful mage.

"Those are your emotions talking for you," Logan said wryly.

Kara winced. He was right. "Look, we were chosen for this quest and now I'm stuck. I'll never find out exactly what we're meant to do unless you help me."

Logan leaned back, placing his fingertips together. "I can't say I'm sorry you came all this way for nothing. But it can't be done."

"Why not?" she demanded.

"The nine crystals were forged long ago. There is no way I can duplicate the enchantment or material exactly."

Kara felt panic setting in. If Logan couldn't help her, the entire quest would fail because she couldn't control her magic. She could not accept that. But what was she going to do?

"However ..." Logan's eyes twinkled as he turned the power crystal over in his hand.

Kara looked up expectantly.

"I *can* provide you with a shell, something that can hold the same amount of magic as a power crystal. It might serve as a temporary replacement. Enough to do the job, anyway."

"Really?" she asked hopefully.

"But you can't enchant it using mage magic."

"What do you mean?"

Lyra bristled. *"He's talking about dark magic."*

Logan grinned. "I can teach you what you need to know."

"What, you mean act like the Dark Sorceress? Forget it."

Logan's eyes turned icy. "The Dark Sorceress is a vicious changeling whose brutality is matched only by her twisted addiction to magic. Hardly my style."

Kara calmed. To her surprise, she believed Logan.

"There isn't just light and dark magic. In between there is shadow," the young man continued. "I'm not evil just because I study arcane arts, and you're not good just because you use mage magic."

Kara blushed. "You're right. I'm sorry. So if it doesn't

matter to you who controls the web, why not just help me save Avalon?"

He stood, smoothing his spotless jacket over his lean figure. "You intrigue me, Kara Davies, blazing star."

"That's because I'm totally intriguing." She got to her feet. Logan was taller than she expected. She had to look up to see into those dark eyes.

"I'll help you. But don't let it get around. It might tarnish my image."

"Kara, I don't like this," Lyra hissed, standing in Kara's path.

"Are you afraid to learn more about magic?" His eyes were impossible to resist. "You are perfectly safe. And you have powerful protectors."

Kara crouched by Lyra. "If I don't follow Mr. Congeniality, I can't replace the power crystal," she whispered. "Besides, I saved the Fairy Realms, I have a power crystal, the best paladin ever, and you guys, what could possibly harm me?"

"Nothing," Goldie chirped.

Lyra growled.

"Just chill." Kara brushed past Lyra and followed Logan across the dance floor toward the back of the club. She would see this through. Logan was going to help her make another power crystal, and that was all that mattered.

There was something cat-like about the fairy's long strides as he guided Kara toward a black door studded with brass spikes. Another pair of stone bouncers guarded the entrance, stepping aside as Logan waved his hand.

"Come. Let me show you what I do," he smiled as the door swung open.

There was something about his confident demeanor that put her at ease. He was a lot like her, she realized. Still, as she stepped into the mysterious chamber, a shadow of doubt gave her pause. She shuddered. What was she getting into?

It would all be worth it in the end, Kara assured herself as she descended into darkness.

18

"*T*HEN THERE WAS *the time I fought the giant squid,*" Gwyx boasted as he glided alongside Drake.

"*Wow, a giant squid.*" The younger dragon hung on the other's every word.

Gwyx had been bragging incessantly since they left the desert. The arid landscape had given way to high, forested plateaus full of tall redwoods and rocky cliffs. Gwyx had first found the shadow dragon in a cave somewhere in these mountains. He was sure it had returned and was holed up there, hoarding its prized power crystal.

"*That feat was only matched by my victory over the demon lord, Fuzzlebub,*" Gwyx droned on.

Ignoring the black dragon, Adriane hunkered down

against Drake's neck, her cheeks flushed with anger. "That Kara has some nerve. She just cut us off!"

Fred huffed indignantly from Adriane's pocket.

Zipping her leather jacket tight against the winds, Adriane glanced over her shoulder at Dreamer. The mistwolf poked his head out of his basket. He understood her thoughts. It was bad enough that Kara had abandoned the unicorns when they were in danger. Now she was hanging out at some fairy mall instead of taking a power crystal back to The Garden. Adriane sensed there must be more to that power crystal than the blazing star had told them, which meant she was hiding something. Kara was acting more and more like the spoiled, too-popular-for-her-own-good golden girl Adriane had first met. That girl had taken magic for herself, not caring that her actions put everyone else in danger. She would have done anything to get what she wanted. Adriane tightened her grip on Drake's reins. The real question was: why? What did Kara want?

"If you don't stand with the pack, you are a danger to the pack," Dreamer said.

Adriane nodded grimly. Dreamer was right. As pack-leader, she knew how important it was to stand together. If Kara had gone rogue, she was a danger to everyone, including herself.

Totally oblivious, Gwyx swept low over the trees, startling a herd of silvery deer. *"Look, brother!"*

"Ooo, pretty," Drake hummed.

"I'm hungry. Let's go rip the head off that doe."

"That is so mean!"

Gwyx turned his purple eyes to Drake. *"What do you eat, then?"*

"Wheat noodles and vegetables ..."

"What are you, a cow?"

"With extra spicy Ak sauce!" Drake retorted.

Gwyx snorted. *"Your contact with humans has dulled your instincts. You know nothing about the warrior code."*

"And what's that?" Adriane was suddenly paying attention to the dragon braggart.

"Eat or be eaten."

Dreamer grinned. *"You have a point there."*

Adriane thought for a moment. "Does this shadow dragon live by the warrior's code too?"

Gwyx's eyes flared. *"The beast has no honor."*

"Where did it come from?"

"The story of the shadow dragon is told to every hatchling." Gwyx spit a lick of flame. *"There was a time, long ago, when dragons bonded with humans, imprinting themselves upon mages as soon as they hatched. But a great dragon warrior was horribly cursed by his bonded."*

"Cursed?" Adriane found this hard to believe.

"The human turned against his dragon," Gwyx growled. *"Selling his own bonded for its magic! So great was the betrayal, the dragon's heart was twisted to utter blackness. He became the shadow creature, a monster whose only desire was to steal the magic of all dragons until not one hatchling*

was left alive. To escape the beast's wrath, the dragons fled to this hidden world and shunned all contact with humans."

Adriane let the tragic story sink in. "That's why Drake is the only dragon anyone's ever seen."

"And will be the last if I don't stop the beast from finding Dragon Home."

"So how did the shadow dragon find your world after all this time?"

Gwyx's eyes flashed in anger. *"Someone has summoned it. The elders suspect a human is out to destroy us."*

Adriane frowned. "What human would even know the shadow dragon existed, much less how to summon it?"

Gwyx roared. *"Such is the way of humans. Lies, deceit, and betrayal mark their history. Now humans want to destroy us and the shadow dragon is their greatest weapon. Being of right age and sound mind, the task has fallen to me to slay this foul beast. It is my warrior quest."*

"Humans aren't all bad," Drake protested. *"My mama is human, and I am bonded to Zach, a mage."*

"No dragon is safe," Gwyx insisted. *"You have already been corrupted by your pitiful humans. You are nothing like other dragons."*

"If they're anything like you, then I'm glad!" Drake snorted.

"Oh really, well—" Gwyx suddenly stopped short, a look of terror glazing his purple eyes.

"What is it?" Adriane nudged Drake close to the black dragon.

"The beast is near." Gwyx flew in a tight circle, scanning the trees below.

"Take us down, Drake."

Wind whipped Adriane's long hair as Drake sailed toward the forest floor. The red dragon landed smoothly in a small clearing among towering trees.

Adriane hopped down from the saddle, removed her flying goggles and checked her silver wolf stone. Nothing. She couldn't sense any magic at all.

"Dreamer?"

The black mistwolf sniffed the air all around them, trying to pick up the magical scent. After a minute he shrugged a wolfish shrug.

"There." Gwyx motioned with his snout. His purple eyes glinted in the shadows of the huge redwoods. The tree line stopped where a sheer rocky cliff surged from the forest like a massive wave. In the stony cliff face, a cave yawned into total blackness. Adriane followed Gwyx's nervous gaze. Inside that cave lay the shadow dragon, and with it, the power crystal.

"We have to move fast, before it detects us," Adriane ordered, then remembered to defer to Gwyx. "Would you lead us, great warrior?"

"Rrrrrr," Gwyx rumbled, shuffling from foot to foot. *"I suppose you have a plan?"*

"Stealth is our only chance," Adriane said. "We have to avoid a fight at all costs. We sneak in, grab the jewel and hightail it out."

"I agree." Gwyx nodded emphatically.

The warrior retied her pony tail, revealing a nervous blue dragonfly hiding on her shoulder. "Fred, you gonna be all right?"

The blue dragonfly looked uncertain.

"If it gets too rough, you go tell the others." She gave the brave little fairy dragon a kiss. "Okay, Team Wolf, let's do it."

Gwyx wavered. *"But do you not think the beast will see—"*

In a swirl of sparkling magic, Dreamer shimmered into a cloud of mist. Suddenly Adriane and Drake disappeared.

Gwyx's eyes went wide.

"We're right here." Drake's big red head suddenly materialized in front of Gwyx's nose.

"By the great wyvern! Of course! Mistwolf magic will shield us."

"The shadow dragon won't see us, but we'll see it," Adriane explained.

Dreamer's mist quivered. *"It's there, I can feel it!"*

"How?" the warrior asked. She still wasn't picking up anything.

"When I take mist form, I can track the shadow creature."

Adriane's jewel flashed as she connected to her packmate. Instantly, cold fire spiked at her senses, filling her with an icy dread. The shadow dragon was powerful, even at this distance. She didn't want to think what it would feel like once they came face to face.

"Move it, Gwyx," Adriane ordered.

The warrior dragon obeyed warily, allowing himself to be hidden under Dreamer's mist.

Positioning herself between the two dragons, Adriane admitted that she wasn't sure how she was going to protect her friends—or herself—if the creature unleashed a full attack. If it came down to a fight, she only hoped Gwyx fought half as well as he talked. Fleeing was not an option.

"We'll need complete silence once we're inside," Adriane instructed the dragons. "Dreamer's mist will absorb most of the noise, but step lightly and stick together."

She could feel Gwyx's body trembling with anxiety.

"Easy," she patted the black dragon gently. "We'll get through this just fine. We'll have the crystal before the shadow dragon even knows we're there."

"Right," Drake agreed.

Gwyx edged closer to the younger red dragon.

"Hammer time!"

The dragons marched in sync toward the dark cave. Aside from the dirt being dislodged, no one would have known they were there, thanks to the magic of the mistwolf.

"Perhaps I should stay by the entrance and prevent its escape," Gwyx whispered nervously.

"We stick together," Adriane ordered.

The open cave gaped before them like a black maw waiting to swallow its prey. *"Rrrrrr, there's something I should tell you—"*

"Stow it." Adriane gave Gwyx a shove as the group entered the cave. Obsidian-flecked walls gleamed, as if the mountain were watching them with dozens of flashing black eyes.

A ferocious growl rumbled from the depths below.

Cold, black power pierced Dreamer's mist like a hundred electric shocks.

Gwyx shook, a small whimper mewling from his throat.

Adriane's stomach turned. An awful dread enveloped her, making her skin crawl, every instinct screaming at her to run away.

Fight it! She commanded herself. Protect the pack at all costs!

The cave floor slanted sharply, taking them deeper and deeper. The dragons walked slowly. They too were fighting the disorienting pull of the darkness below.

Adriane pushed on, magic vibrating through her like thunder. They were getting close.

Gwyx stopped suddenly and pointed a trembling wingtip.

Pale light played over gleaming walls of a giant underground cavern. There, dead center, the shadow dragon lay coiled on a flat rock, rippling scales of smoke and

shadow undulating. The creature was larger than Gwyx or Drake. And unlike those real dragons, this one was not solid. A nightmarish apparition of dragon magic, the creature's long spiked neck snaked from a shifting, ghostlike body. Giant wings fluttered like specters, teeth and claws appearing and disappearing like avenging spirits.

Adriane stood stone still.

The beast suddenly lifted its massive head. Eyes like livid coals glowed in the darkness, sweeping the cave with a hunter's glare. Its black forked tongue shot from its mouth, tasting the air for intruders. The beast knew something was in its lair, even if it couldn't see them.

But all Adriane could see was the glowing object throbbing like a wicked heart inside the monster's chest. Shadowy red and purple radiated from the crystal in hypnotic waves. At once the warrior knew she'd have to change her plan. She couldn't just sneak up and snatch the power crystal; it had merged with the creature. To get her prize, she was going to have to slay the dragon.

Tapping her dragons on their wings, she gave them the silent signal to advance. Surprise was the only advantage they had.

The creature shifted, blood-red eyes darting around the cave. Adriane steeled herself. They would have only precious seconds before the beast discovered them.

They were almost there. Adriane raised her wrist, preparing to—

With a blood-curdling shriek, the shadow dragon struck like a viper. To Adriane's shock, it lunged past the group. A second noise ricocheted off the walls behind her, rocketing into a deafening chorus of fear.

"Gwyx!" Drake cried.

Adriane whipped around and saw Gwyx standing—completely visible—at the cavern's entrance. He had been too frightened to move.

"mama." Gwyx cowered as the shadow dragon attacked in a storm of dagger claws and razor teeth.

Snorting fire, Drake charged into battle, knocking Gwyx away from danger. With a terrible shriek the shadow dragon turned its rage on the red dragon.

Adriane leaped through the air, Dreamer snarling at her side. Silver fire burst from her wolf stone, lassoing the shadow dragon's neck. With all of her strength, Adriane yanked the beast away from Drake. The monster spun around, its blazing eyes boring into Adriane like an iron spike of pure terror.

She collapsed to the ground, her mouth open in a silent scream. Paralyzed, she could only watch in horror as the monster pounded into Dreamer, crushing the mistwolf with nightmarish power.

Fighting to stay conscious, the howls and screams of her friends filled her head with unbearable agony. Her worst fears were unfolding horrifically in front of her. Her pack was dying, and she was powerless to do anything!

"No!" she cried.

Adriane was the packleader. She would fight to the death to defend her pack. Survival was as instinctual as breathing. Desperately, she reached out to the strongest member of her pack.

A silver spark flashed from her jewel. For a second it was as if she stood on the highest hill of the Ravenswood Preserve, the green meadows and thick forests surrounding her. The preserve's pure magic engulfed her as the great forest protector, Stormbringer, her paladin, filled her with strength.

Snarling, she staggered to her feet. Nothing was going to harm her packmates while she had even an ounce of strength to fight.

The spark raged into a flame, filling the cave with slivers of light. Power rushed though Adriane like a raging river. Throwing back her head, she howled with feral fury, and let the wolf inside run free.

In a flash of silver, Adriane dissolved into mist.

Whipping past the shadow dragon's claws, she dove into the beast, wrapping herself around its pulsing, crystalline heart. Dark magic twisted through her every molecule, crackling like lightning as she wrenched the power crystal away.

The cave went suddenly, eerily quiet.

"Where did it go?" Gwyx cried, his frightened eyes darting around the cavern.

The shadow dragon had vanished!

Through heightened wolf eyes, Adriane surveyed the cave. Dreamer stood by her side. Drake sat next to Gwyx, looking dazed. There was no sign of the fearsome shadow beast.

"It needed the power crystal to stay alive," she said, gasping with the effort of morphing back into solid human form. She felt weird, as if her physical body no longer anchored her, as if she was in deep space, floating away into blackness.

"*Packmate.*" Dreamer stared up at her, his gaze moving left and right, not quite finding her eyes.

Gwyx stepped forward, stretching his wings. "*You can come out now, human Adriane. I have slain the shadow dragon!*"

"You didn't slay anything, and I'm right here."

"*No you're not.*" Dreamer's emerald eyes flashed with fear.

Startled, Adriane looked down at her hands and feet. She could only see a faint ghost-like outline of her body.

"*The magic is inside you,*" Dreamer said.

Adriane stared in horror at the power crystal. It throbbed in the center of her chest, beating like a black heart, pulsing shadow magic through her veins. Squeezing her eyes shut, she tried again to turn back to solid form.

After a few seconds, she took a deep breath, opened her eyes and held her hand in front of her face. She could see the dragons and Dreamer right through her invisible hand.

"I—I 'm stuck."

Dreamer circled her, trying to help her with his magic. *"You can't stay in mist form, it's too dangerous!"*

A memory struck Adriane, and she gulped. The Dark Sorceress had nearly exterminated the mistwolves by trapping them in mist form. If she couldn't turn solid again soon, both she and the power crystal would drift away into nothingness. Time was critical.

She cried out as the black magic tightened its grip. It would take all her strength to fight the crystal. And it wasn't a fight she could win.

"Dreamer, what do I do?" Panic twisted her stomach.

"We must run the Spirit Trail to Packhome," Dreamer declared. *"We need the full power of the pack to help you."*

"Well, I'll just leave you to your little problems." Gwyx strutted toward the mouth of the cave. *"I've completed my quest, and I must return home to tell the elders that I have saved everyone."*

Suddenly Drake rushed after Gwyx. *"I will accompany you."*

"Excellent!" Gwyx stopped in mid step. *"You can bear witness to my daring exploits."*

Adriane tried to steady herself. "Are you sure, Drake?"

"Of course. I cannot travel on the Spirit Trail." Drake swished his long tail.

Adriane had been forced to let her first bonded wolf, Stormbringer, go to find her pack. It looked like Drake had the same opportunity now that he, too, knew there were others of his kind.

"Just let me do the talking," Gwyx advised. *"I wouldn't want you to stick your tail in your mouth the first time you met the elders."*

"Agreed," Drake nodded.

"And I wouldn't mention anything about being bonded to all these humans."

"I will say nothing about the girl." Drake's yellow eyes swept over the space where Adriane stood. *"I mean Mama."*

Adriane snarled as the dark power writhed inside her. She couldn't take Drake with her, even if he'd wanted to go. "I'll check in from Packhome."

"Good," Drake approved.

"Hurry, Dreamer." Adriane reached out to her pack-mate, preparing to use another of her Level Two talents. She and Dreamer were world walkers and could run the Spirit Trail, the mystical pathway of the mistwolves that would lead them to Packhome.

Dreamer stood, eye closed, summoning the magic that would open the passage between worlds. Blue light shimmered around mistwolf and warrior as they moved from the physical world and onto the astral planes of magic.

Adriane glanced over her shoulder as the cave fell away, but Drake had already left with Gwyx. Swallowing hard, she and Dreamer stepped as one onto the ancient Spirit Trail and vanished.

19

"**O**ZZIE!" EMILY SCREAMED for her friend as swirling lights swam before her eyes.

"Emily, it's okay."

The healer blinked at the familiar voice. She suddenly realized she was leaning against something purple and soft. She took a step back and gazed into a pair of deep blue eyes.

"Indi!" She threw her arms around her paladin's strong neck, burying her face in his soft mane.Indigo was a magnificent unicorn, created from the magic of the only living power crystal, the Heart of Avalon.

Sensing her danger, Indi must have opened a magical doorway at the bottom of the gully and pulled her to safety. Unicorns were one of the only animals that could open portals at will.

The ground beneath her swayed, throwing her off balance.

She gasped. Green pathways stretched all around her, woven together so tightly she could barely see through them. The Spider Witch's web.

The magic of the Otherworlds clung to the web in gleaming deposits like dew. The awful truth was right before her eyes. She had connected the Otherworlds to the Spider Witch's web.

Suddenly tears were streaming down her cheeks. The healer buried her face in Indi's neck.

"Indi, I've done something terrible," Emily cried, her words coming out in a jumble. "I connected the Otherworlds to this web and Ozzie and Lorren, I left them, and we were attacked by a pack of shadow creatures…"

Indi leaned his head over her shoulder in a unicorn hug. *"I saw Ozzie and Lorren go through another portal."*

Emily let out a huge sigh of relief. Her friends had made it through Tweek's portal. They were safe. She tried to steady herself as the web swayed again. Her jewel burned with the power of the Otherworld's dark magic. She looked away, her eyes flinching against the pain.

"I have to fix it!" she blurted.

"I will help you." Indi's magic rushed through her,

warm and soothing. *"But you must heal yourself before you can heal others."*

Gulping back tears, Emily raised her wrist. Rainbow magic flowed from Indi's crystal horn, entwining with her blue healing light. The magic wrapped around her body like sunlight. Slowly, her scratches and scrapes melted away, her bruises faded, and the throbbing pain in her ankle subsided, then vanished.

The Spider Witch's magic grated against Emily as she examined the tangled web. The grid-like pattern was much more rigid than the other section of the magic web Emily had seen. Suddenly she realized what the witch had done. With the skill of a spider, she had unraveled the existing magic web and woven it into her own dark design.

Emily's eyes widened. There was something else, a familiar silver aura underneath. The original web was still there! A bright flash of hope flared through her jewel. As long as that magic existed, there was a chance she could undo the witch's weaving. She'd just returned the web to its original form in the kobold's home.

But healing the entire web was an enormous task. She needed more magic.

"Over there." Indi pointed his horn.

Emily squinted. A splash of glittering red bobbed on the horizon. The power crystal!

Grasping the unicorn's mane, Emily jumped onto his back. "Let's go!"

With a toss of his head, Indi galloped down the magical pathway, sparks flying off his hooves. Emily leaned into her paladin's neck as he charged toward the glowing jewel.

Raising her wrist, she flung a strand of bright blue magic at the crystal, trying to ensnare it. But just as before, the power crystal floated away.

Sensing her urgency, Indi picked up speed. The unicorn leaped over strands of glowing green as he chased the power crystal along its twisting course, always just out of reach.

In a flash, it disappeared.

"Follow it!" Emily cried.

Horn blazing with power, Indi opened a portal. White light rushed past Emily as they careened through the magical doorway.

Emily pitched forward as Indi skidded to a stop, hooves scrambling at the edge of a rocky precipice. She shifted her weight back, helping her paladin regain his balance.

"What is this?" the healer breathed, wind whipping at her curls.

An enormous gorge with sheer walls gaped before them. The bottom was shrouded in thick gray mist. And in the center of the abyss, an immense castle rose on a rocky pedestal. Stone turrets curled to the gray skies like giant insect legs. There were no doors or windows. Not even a bridge to reach the castle. At least no bridge a girl and her unicorn could use. Instead, strands of glowing, green web served as bridges for hundreds of hideous spiders. They skittered back and forth like ants in a colony, each driven by its own secret purpose.

The Spider Witch's lair.

Power pulsed from every stone of the imposing castle, as if some ancient evil were waiting to be set free from its dark interior.

There was another concentration of magic nearby, something so familiar, like a faint melody. Emily's pulse quickened. Beneath the rays of swirling black power, she sensed it: unicorns!

"Lorelei!" Emily used her telepathic power to call to her friend.

But there was no answer.

"The power crystal must have been drawn to the unicorns." Emily's heart skipped a beat.

"I can feel them!" Indi stamped his hooves.

The Spider Witch had the missing unicorns as well as the power crystal in her clutches!

"Fiona," Emily called, willing the tiny dragonfly to appear and send a message to Adriane, Dreamer, Kara, Lyra, and Ozzie.

But the red d-fly either couldn't hear her or was too frightened to come near the Spider Witch's lair.

Emily took a deep breath. It was up to them.

"Can you get us inside?" She stroked Indi's neck.

He lowered his head, pointing his horn toward the towering castle.

Emily's stomach flipped as her paladin leaped off the precipice. The gorge tilted below them, jagged rocks piercing the fog like teeth.

In a flash, they landed in darkness. Everything was eerily quiet.

She patted Indi to keep him still while her eyes adjusted. They were deep within the lair, its massive weight pressing down on them as if they were inside a tomb. Murky yellow crystals set in the walls illuminated a cavernous room. In the corners, pools of black swallowed the dim light.

The place may have looked deserted but Emily knew instantly it was not.

"Healer."

Something moved in the dank shadows. Something that knew her.

Slipping from Indi's back, Emily crept forward. "Lorelei?"

"Come closer," the unicorn's voice rasped.

Fear tingled up Emily's spine. She recognized the voice of her unicorn friend, but something about it was off. "Are you hurt?" Emily held up her jewel, sending a beam of light into the shadows.

"Lorelei!" Emily gasped.

Instead of the pure white unicorn that Emily knew and loved, the creature before her had transformed. Lorelei's horn blazed with red magic, and her warm golden eyes were glazed sickly yellow. Even her snow-white coat was dull and grayish.

"What happened to you?" Emily whispered, horrified. Her stomach twisted with pain as she searched for Lorelei's strong, pure aura. What she saw sickened her. The unicorn's magic had been rewoven, tainted with dark red.

"Emily."

The healer whipped around, jewel light slicing through the gloom. Dozens of unicorns, all with twisted, red magic gleaming from their proud crystal horns converged on her.

"Pollo, Riannan?" Emily reached out to the unicorn prince and princess, her eyes filled with tears.

"We have been waiting for you, healer."

The unicorns surrounded her, their once-sparkling eyes now glowing evilly. She felt as if she would suffocate as their dark magic engulfed her.

"Lead us, dark witch."

Frantically, Emily sent her healing magic billowing over the unicorns. But the new weaving was knotted too tight, it wouldn't budge. Only a master weaver could have captured creatures as powerful as unicorns.

"Indi, help!" Emily cried.

"Your paladin can not help you, healer."

Emily staggered back, horrified by the figure emerging from the shadows.

Dark hood pulled over her head, her spider body hidden by a flowing black robe, the witch slowly advanced. In her pale, veiny hands, a large crystal glowed red—the power crystal they'd been chasing! Tendrils of magic arced from the witch's bony fingers, flaring over the unicorns and—

"Indi!" Emily screamed.

But Indi could not hear her. The mighty paladin stood transfixed as strands of sticky green webbing slithered around his body, draping over him in a darkly gleaming net. The unicorn's bright rainbow horn swirled to red as he too fell prey to the witch's weaving.

"No!" Emily lashed out, trying to sever the witch's magic. But she was no match for the master weaver.

The Spider Witch's faceted insect eyes glinted with pleasure. "Right on time, little fly."

20

"WELCOME TO MY world," Logan said proudly.

Kara stared at the fairy's enormous underground workshop. It looked like he had combined Frankenstein's laboratory with a magic shop.

Hanging crystals cast steel-blue light over a long chrome table crowded with supplies. Bunsen burners, scales, jars of what Kara hoped weren't tiny eyeballs, and bundles of dried herbs, all gathered in separate clumps as if Logan were working on several projects at once. Tall shelves crammed with ancient leather bound books lined three walls. Along the fourth wall, neatly labeled glass cabinets gleamed with swirling potions, talismans, and various jewels.

Everything seemed neatly organized, groups of gross-looking things over there, glowing ugly things here, vials with potions, skulls, and a few dried bats hanging over there.

"Are you a sculptor, too?" Kara circled a dozen statues that looked similar to the stone guards in the club. Some were missing an arm, leg, or hand, while a few resembled molten lumps of clay. The blazing star could just imagine Logan down here late at night sculpting these things like a mad genius.

Lyra's sharp cat eyes watched Logan's every move.

"I am quite the artist," Logan said proudly. "These are golems." He patted an armless giant. "With the right spell I bring them to life, as you saw."

"You really are Dr. Frankenstein," Kara commented.

"That guy was an amateur," Logan scoffed. "Everyone knows if you try to raise the dead you only get a zombie."

"Duh." Kara rolled her eyes. "So you use warlock magic to make golems, then."

"Some. Mostly I use alchemy—the science of transforming one thing into another," Logan explained. "Not quite the fireworks of a blazing star, but much more precise. When I animate these rock guards, I know exactly what's going to happen. All I need is the right ingredients, patience, and careful planning."

"Quite the gourmet."

"Exactly." Logan's voice was like warm honey.

Kara liked the fact that Logan could get what he wanted, when he wanted it. It was like using her wishing crystal.

"So maybe I should learn more about arcane magic," she said coyly.

Lyra growled.

"Shhh, not now," Kara whispered.

She leaned in close to him, brushing against a strange, gleaming cage. "So tell me more."

"I wouldn't stand too close to—"

Kara reeled as something inside shrieked and slammed against the cage door.

Her unicorn jewel showered blood-red sparks as the creature viciously latched onto her magic. Lights flashed in front of her eyes as her unicorn jewel dimmed like a dying flame.

Lyra rushed to her aid, teeth bared.

Kara jerked back, severing the creature's greedy hold on her jewel. She had never felt anything like its icy magic. Instinctively she knew the creature would have drained every last spark of her magic if she had let it.

"Are you all right?" Logan reached out to steady her.

"What's in there?" she breathed, pushing hair from her face.

"A shadow creature."

Strengthened by the blazing star's magic, a shape materialized. The ghostly gargoyle slinked in and out of sight, sharp wingtips, long teeth, and razor claws glistening. The creature growled menacingly as it pulsed in and out of solid form.

"*It attacked her!*" Lyra snarled.

"The blazing star is more than a match for one little shadow creature."

"How come it went after my magic like that?"

"That's what a shadow creature does. It's a magic parasite, sucking magic until the host dies."

"What are you doing with it?" Kara asked.

"Special order for a client. I designed this cage to hold it," he bragged.

Kara watched the creature disappear into smoke.

"Ah, here we go." The warlock pointed behind her. A large black cabinet with a strange padlock loomed in the shadows. "Crystal ingredients are in there."

Kara put her hand on the crystal knob. It was locked.

"Only I can open that. Anyone else who touches it will grow six horns on their elbow."

Kara jumped back, horrified.

"Kidding," Logan chuckled.

"Oh, that's hilarious."

Logan raised his pale hands. Tendrils of silver magic zapped from his fingertips, opening the door. Inside were glowing boxes, velvet sacks, and carefully wrapped ingredients. It all looked extremely valuable.

"*Kara, I don't like this.*" Lyra pressed against Kara's side. "*He's trying to make you use dark magic.*"

"Chill, kitty cat." Logan closed the cabinet, holding

an armful of supplies. "Magic is just a tool to get what we want. Kara wants to open the Gates of Avalon, and arcane magic can make another power crystal. Simple."

"Exactly," Kara agreed.

Lyra growled, not convinced.

A sudden flare of anger flushed Kara's cheeks as she turned on Lyra. "This is our chance to replace the power crystal. Don't you want to get into Avalon?"

The cat's emerald eyes flickered. *"You shouldn't be experimenting alone. You, Emily, and Adriane can make this crystal together."*

"I'm going to get everything I want right here, right now, and you want me to wait so those two can yell at me again? I don't think so." Kara glared at her bonded. "A little support from you wouldn't hurt, either. What? Now *you* don't you trust me either?"

"Magic has a price," Lyra replied evenly. *"This is too dangerous for you."*

Furious, Kara stalked away, leaving Goldie and Lyra alone. Her desire for the power crystal burned inside her. Why was it that none of her friends ever supported her when she needed it? Replacing this crystal would not only get them into Avalon, it would prove once and for all that she was a good mage, a great mage, the best mage! And if Lyra, her best friend, didn't understand, well, Kara had just made a new friend.

"The cat has a point." Logan's smooth voice said. The fairy was standing close beside her. "Magic does have a price. The question is, are you willing to pay it to get what you want?"

The wishing crystal glowed, filling her with confidence.

Kara glanced at Lyra. Goldie perched on the cat's head. They seemed to be whispering to one another. What were they discussing? She had the sneaking suspicion they were plotting against her, trying to stop her from working with Logan.

"I'll do whatever it takes," Kara stated.

Logan smiled his devastating smile. "Then let's do it."

She followed him to the worktable and helped him lay out the supplies. He pulled a wide chrome basin from a shelf beneath the table.

"I anodized this myself with a special anti-corrosion spell," Logan informed her.

"Cool." Who knew Logan would turn out to be such a brain? Maybe it was time to see what else he knew. "So why are you helping me open the Gates of Avalon, really?"

"You see all those books? Not one of them says a thing about the power crystals," Logan said. "Strange, isn't it? The most famous gems in the world, and there's not even an honorable mention. Seems like whoever made them wanted to keep it a secret. I, for one, would like to know what's inside the gates."

Kara nodded, suddenly feeling nervous.

"What?"

"It's just that I still don't really know what's going to happen," she burst out. "We get nine crystals to this weird tropical island, and then what? Nobody can tell us anything."

"The true nature of what lies inside Avalon is one of the great mysteries of the web." Logan smiled reassuringly. "Trust your instincts. You'll know what to do."

Lyra and Goldie approached the table, watching Logan like a pair of hawks. The fairy untied a velvet pouch and poured out a palm full of glittering red sand.

"Iridium," Logan explained, pouring the fine dust onto a silver scale. "A powerful bonding element. Every magic jewel has some iridium."

"What's all the other stuff?"

"Mithril, agate, quartz, essence of fire." Logan tossed the ingredients into the chrome basin as he named them off.

"So we say abracadabra and then I've got a power crystal?"

"Only the shell. You're going to need a magical creature to fill it."

"How about Goldie?" Kara suggested.

Logan grinned at the little dragon. "No offense, short stuff, but this isn't just any jewel, it's a power crystal. You need a strong power source to give it some oomph. A group of unicorns might do it."

Kara scowled as Lyra looked at her pointedly. "I can't find any unicorns."

"How about some mistwolves?" Logan suggested.

"They're spread out all over Aldenmor."

Logan thought for a moment. "A dragon would definitely do it, but what dragon is going to help you? They're extinct."

Kara's eyes opened wide. "I know a dragon. He loves me!"

"You're full of surprises, star."

"That's why I'm so popular."

"Putting dragon magic in this shell is only a temporary fix," Logan warned. "It'll be as strong as a power crystal, but only for a little while. You must be in place and ready to use it as soon as you get the magical charge."

"Can't you make it last longer?"

Logan shook his head. "Afraid not."

"Fine, I'll have to do it at the gates, then."

Rrrrring.

Goldie shook her head. "Not me."

"Excuse me." Logan flipped open his slim black cell phone. "Yes?"

Giving Kara an apologetic look, he wandered to the other side of the chamber to talk in private, leaving the three alone.

Lyra nudged Kara. *"He's not telling you something, Kara, this isn't good. Let's go. Now!"*

"No dark magic," Goldie huffed.

"You guys sound just like Emily and Adriane!" Anger flooded Kara's senses. "I figure out how to make the missing crystal and you're scolding me!"

It was so frustrating, Kara thought as she watched the unicorn power crystal glow in her hand. None of her supposed friends ever wanted to let her do what she needed to do.

"Wish us out of here," Lyra insisted.

"Fine." Kara's hand closed around the unicorn power crystal. She was running out of time. "I wish you guys would go back to Ravenswood."

In a flash, her two bondeds disappeared.

Logan strode across the room, slipping his cell phone back into his pocket. "I told my client she'd have to wait because I have a very important guest." He scanned his workshop. "Where'd Sylvester and Tweety go?"

"Oh, I sent them home." She smiled as he arched a perfect eyebrow. "I know, pretty dramatic, but I'll catch up with them later. They just don't understand. Not like you do."

"That's another problem with mage magic: Everybody's always giving you their opinion." Logan poured the gleaming iridium into his palm. "Magic is fluid, constantly in motion, constantly changing, whether we realize it or not. You have to know what you want and go for it." He paused, a palm full of iridium balanced over the chrome basin. "You ready?"

"Absolutely." Kara's eyes sparkled with glee. This was exactly what she wanted.

Logan let the iridium fall in a glittering shower.

He reached his hand out to her.

Kara placed her hand in his, flushing.

"To get the strongest crystal, we must imbue these ingredients with a fiery enchantment."

"Fire, that's me," Kara whispered.

Logan pulled her closer, looking deep into her eyes. "You must be very careful. Let your emotions take over, and the spell is ruined. You'll create something you don't want. You must be calm, cool, completely in control."

"I'm cool," Kara assured him.

Logan bent his head. When he looked up, his eyes seemed even blacker, huge dark moons in his pale face. He began chanting in a strange language she had never heard before. The basin glowed as the ingredients bubbled, then swirled into a tiny vortex.

"Showtime." Logan plunged their clasped hands into the whirling spell.

Steel gray magic crackled from his fingertips, mingling with the fire erupting from Kara's fingers. The spell instantly latched onto her magic, its pull more voracious than the starved shadow creature. Sweat prickled her forehead as she fought the instinct to pull back. She wanted this, she reminded herself, and forced her magic to flow freely.

Struggling to keep her emotions under control, she gasped as a form began to take shape in the roiling magic.

Wisps of red and pink and silver melted into hard flat shapes.

"Steady, we're almost there," Logan said calmly.

The little pieces spun in a tight circle, clicking together to create a perfect golden gem with gleaming facets. It was done. Kara whooped, unable to maintain her cool any longer.

The power crystal was hers at last.

21

$\mathcal{E}$MILY HAD WALKED right into a trap. She stared in disbelief at the immense tapestry hanging from the wall in the Spider Witch's vast chamber.

The design on it was an image of the entire web, every tiny strand intricately woven into place. It didn't look like the free-flowing map that Tasha had displayed on the library ceiling. Instead of glittering loops and swirls, the tapestry's version had sharply defined lines in diamond and square shaped patterns. It felt cold and lifeless. A monstrous aberration, just like its creator.

"Magnificent, isn't it?" The Spider Witch gazed at her masterpiece, the power crystal glowing in her hands.

Emily stiffened as the unicorns gathered closer, their horns flashing erratically, strobing the room with crimson. Indi stood in their midst, trapped like the others in the witch's spell.

"Let them go!" Emily demanded. Indi's twisted aura cut through her senses like a knife. She tried to focus as the walls tilted, colors dripping like blood.

"I've had experience entrapping paladins." The witch emitted a clicking sound like grating laughter. "You can see for yourself that he and the other unicorns have not been harmed."

Not physically, anyway. But the witch had twisted their pure magical auras into a pattern of her own design. Her heart ached to help them.

"I should thank you, healer. It's been a long time since the Otherworlds have been a part of the web." The witch pointed a long finger at a glowing diamond-shaped green section.

Emily saw how the section fit perfectly into the rest of the tapestry, like a piece of a puzzle. Her face flushed with anger and guilt. "You tricked me."

The witch's yellow eyes glittered from the darkness of her hood. "Yes, I sent the kobolds to you. I knew you could not resist the desire to help them. You are a healer."

Emily eyed the power crystal gleaming in the witch's hands. For the first time, Emily could clearly see the crystal's aura. It radiated murky waves of purple and black. She shivered. "You used that to lure me here."

The witch turned the jewel over in her hands. "Do you know what kind of crystal this is?"

Emily shook her head.

"A healing crystal."

Emily gasped. "How could you use a healing jewel to twist unicorns?"

"It shouldn't surprise you. Healing and weaving are the same thing," the witch said. "When you heal an animal, you are repairing a damaged pattern. When I weave, I am taking a pattern apart and making something new. You understand?"

Emily did understand. Before she could heal any creature, she first had to undo—take away—the illness, or injury.

"What would make the unicorns come to you?" she asked as the unicorns pressed closer. "They would never answer your call."

"That is true." The witch's eyes danced. "But they would answer yours."

Emily furrowed her brow, confused. She hadn't directed them here.

"An easy mistake for a novice to make. The web you made with the sorceress's help summoned all kinds of creatures to your aid."

"I don't understand." Emily thought that web was just a terrible memory.

"My dear healer, a web that powerful continues to radiate magic long after the spell is complete. I simply directed it at the unicorns. They came because *you* summoned them."

Panic spread through Emily's body, escalating with every heartbeat. The web she had made with the help of the Dark Sorceress. So many animals had answered her call because she was the healer and they trusted her. But she had unwittingly betrayed them, giving their magic to the evil sorceress. And now it was all her fault the unicorns had been trapped!

A horrifying thought occurred to her. "All those dark creatures appearing on the web, shadow creatures—my web summoned them, too?"

The witch loomed over her with a sickeningly satisfied smile. "They have all been answering your call."

Emily felt dizzy, as if she were about to pass out. Her whole life, she had worked to help animals and keep them safe. But now she saw how right she had been to fear her magic. Reaching Level Two had spelled disaster for the web, the unicorns, and all the animals that needed magic to survive.

"You've seen for yourself the old web is damaged beyond repair," the Spider Witch said. "My web can replace it. See how perfect my pattern is." The witch indicated her tapestry. "So much improved over the old one."

"What do you need the unicorns for?" Emily demanded.

"The web is only as strong as the magic that flows through it. The unicorns will run the web as they are meant to, but they will spread *my* magic where I want it to go."

"A unicorn's magic can't be taken! And they would never give magic to you."

"But they will give it willingly to you."

Indi leaned his head over Emily's shoulder, his dark aura enveloping her. *"Lead us, healer."*

"The web needs magic," the corrupted unicorns called.

Emily felt overwhelmed. Like a true spider, the witch had set a trap for everything she needed: the unicorns, the Otherworlds, Emily herself.

Repulsed though she was, Emily couldn't help seeing a certain beauty in the work. There was logic, albeit twisted, in what the Spider Witch said. Emily had seen the extensive damage on the magic web. Maybe it really was beyond repair. She winced. The only thing she was sure of was her need, as a healer, to save the animals at all costs.

"I know you see the beauty of my design," the witch said into her ear. "You are the only one who can truly understand."

Emily studied the tapestry, opening her magical vision. Hidden beneath the witch's cold, angular lines, she could see faint sparkles of looping strands—the original web! She could feel it slipping away like sand. But as long as even a hint of the original web was still there, she could heal it! It was the only shot she had. She didn't have much time. And she'd need all her friends to do it.

Emily tried to play it cool while she formulated a plan. "What do you want from me?" she demanded of her captor.

"There is one last thing I must have to complete my web. No one can find it." The witch ran her hand over the tapestry—"except you."

Emily kept her expression as immobile as stone.

"The Gates of Avalon," the witch pressed. "*You* are connected to it through your paladin, forged from the Heart of Avalon."

"The island?" Emily asked as the final piece of the puzzle fell into place. The witch needed Emily because the healer was the only one who could find the Gates of Avalon, with Indi's guidance.

"It is impossible to locate," the witch continued, "constantly moving, protected by a strong shield, as you know. But your paladin can find it."

"What happened?" Emily asked. "Why did your quest fail?"

"That doesn't matter now." The witch leaned in so close Emily could smell her rancid odor. "You have a chance to save the web. If the unicorns don't spread the magic of Avalon along my web, there will be no magic web at all, and all your little animal friends will die."

Lorelei stepped to Emily's side. "*The animals need us.*"

"*We must run the web,*" the unicorns chorused.

The healer edged back, but Lorelei moved in closer, the other unicorns right behind her.

"*Open the gates.*"

"*Release Avalon's magic for us!*"

If she could get this power crystal to the island, Emily

could heal the web with her friends. She could only pray Adriane, Kara, and Ozzie would find their way and meet her. With all her heart, she believed they would. They just had to be there. She had never needed her friends more than she needed them now.

The witch held out the power crystal to Emily. Shadows shifted across her hazel eyes.

The healer accepted it, her fingers closing around the pulsing gem. "Indi, show me the Gates of Avalon," she commanded.

Magic flashed from his horn, illuminating the exquisite patterns. A brilliant point of light flashed near the edge of the design. Emily knew that aura. It was the Heart of Avalon, the crystal that would guide them to the island.

"At last!" The Spider Witch's insect eyes gleamed as she raised her arms.

Dozens of spiders dropped from the ceiling on glowing silken threads and skittered onto the tapestry. In a frenzy of clicking and hissing, they began to weave.

The Spider Witch's arms swooped through the air like a mad conductor as her spiders wove the elusive Gates of Avalon into the witch's pattern.

The tapestry rippled, strands shifted and finally settled as the Spider Witch's web locked into place.

Colors flared to vibrant life under Emily's magical vision. The witch's web was flawless. The unicorns' auras had been woven as a perfect complement to the new web they would run upon.

"It is done!" the witch cried triumphantly.

The healer grasped the power crystal in trembling hands. Magic flowed through her like dark fire as auras swirled and glowed around her. She wasn't even trying, and she could see the auras of the unicorns, Indi, the tapestry, even the Spider Witch herself.

The unicorns reared and whinnied, eager to run the dark web.

The Spider Witch threw off her black robe and climbed up the tapestry on her eight horrendous spider legs. Reaching into the center of her evil web, she sat like a giant black widow. Glittering insect eyes gleamed at Emily.

"Go, healer. Bring me Avalon."

22

*L*ORREN PACED ALONG a wide strand of glowing green web, the little orange dragonfly, Blaze, perched on his shoulder. The goblin prince and Ozzie had landed on a nexus, a point where several strands of web intersected like crisscrossing railways. A dozen brilliant portals swirled around them.

Lorren had used Blaze to dial up Goldie. But when he discovered she was at Ravenswood, he sent another of the dragonfly crew—purple Barney—to find Kara, and take his magical call. Now he was explaining, "Kara, I was worried about you. That's why I sent Barney."

"Well, that's nice, but I'm fine," Kara snapped.

"Then where's Goldie?" Lorren asked.

"Sent her home."

"You what?"

Ozzie scrambled up the prince's shoulder and shouted into Blaze's belly. "You compost heap! Where's Emily?"

"What?" the blazing star's offended voice asked.

"Ozzie! I'm talking to Kara, not Tweek." He brushed the ferret away, annoyed by the interruption.

Grumbling, the furry mage scowled, trying not to tumble into an open portal as the unstable web rippled beneath his paws. Untethered, tangled strands shifted, snaking into a massive knot of green in the distance. If Emily had been here, as Tweek claimed, she wasn't here now. If that mulch pile let anything happen to her, Ozzie would feed him to the jeeran!

"You don't know where Emily is?" Kara asked.

"Tweek was trying to pop us to her." Lorren paced anxiously.

"What about Xena?"

"She's on her way to the mistwolf packhome. She found a power crystal but—"

"Oh and she yelled at *me* for not taking my crystal to The Garden. She is unbelievable!" Kara ranted. "She'd better pull it together, because I just made a new power crystal."

"You did?" Ozzie ran over. "How?"

"With my new friend."

"And who's that?" Lorren asked.

"If you must know, his name is Logan and he knows everything about every—"

"Logan? The Fairy Underground has a huge file on that guy," Lorren yelled. "He's a dark fairy!"

"So what? You're a goblin. You have something against fairies?"

"No, I mean yes! Kara, Logan is not your friend."

"Well, I like him and I can take care of myself!"

"Oy." Ozzie threw up his arms in frustration as he listened to them.

"Kara, you don't know what you're getting yourself into."

"That's the popular theory."

"You haven't talked to the others, you don't even know what's going on."

"Don't know, don't care."

Fed up, Ozzie stomped away, plopping himself onto a glittery mound. "Great, Lorren's fighting with Kara, Emily's missing, and Adriane's running all over the web. I might as well be talking to myself!"

Twinkling light sparked up Ozzie's spine. He scratched his back and sighed dejectedly. Nobody ever listened to him. But why should they? It wasn't like he was helping on this quest anyway. There was still one more power crystal to find and nobody knew where it was, least of all him.

"I got the lonesome ferret bluewuwuwuwuwuues," Ozzie sang a mournful ballad. "And I don't know what to dowoowoowoowooo—oogAH!"

He leaped to his feet, his fur crackling like a sparkler. "What the—!"

"So because I don't use magic I'm not good enough for you?" Lorren's voice echoed across the stillness of the web.

"I'm the blazing star! I guess you'll never understand."

"Fine!"

"Fine!"

Ozzie furiously tore at the sticky webbing covering the mound he'd been sitting on. Reaching into the wet mass, he pulled out a glittering, goo-covered object. He rubbed it clean with his furry arm, revealing brilliant crystalline facets. His ferret jaw dropped.

"Lorren," he squeaked.

The prince wheeled around, almost tripping over Ozzie

as he yelled into Blaze's belly. "I understand this Logan character, and I don't like you hanging out with him."

"I can't believe you're jealous!" Kara scoffed.

"Lorren!" Ozzie jumped up and down, waving the power crystal.

"I am not jeal—"

Ozzie grabbed Blaze's foot. "Gimme that d-fly!"

"ooowEEwawa!" Blaze stretched like a rubber band.

"Ozzie what are you doing?" Lorren scowled.

"I found a power crystal!" the ferret screamed.

"What? Are you sure?"

Ozzie touched the power crystal to his jewel. Instantly, his fur stuck out like a porcupine.

"Ozzie found the last crystal!" Lorren cried.

"Good work, furball, one less thing for me to do," Kara said. "Thanks for the chat, but I need one last ingredient for this replacement crystal. If Adriane doesn't screw up, we have them all. Later."

"Kara, wait." But she had hung up. Lorren grimaced. "I don't get her."

"She's a teenage girl, don't even try." Ozzie jumped as the power crystal flashed in his hands. "We have to get back to Ravenswood!"

Lorren scanned the dozen doorways swirling dizzyingly around them. "Which one?"

"That one," Ozzie pointed to a swirling circle of light.

"How can you tell?"

Ozzie picked up a packet of trail mix he had carefully

placed when they arrived. "Better than bread crumbs." He dumped the last of the raisins and nuts in his mouth.

"Ozzie, you never cease to amaze me," Lorren exclaimed as he followed the ferret through the doorway.

They tumbled out into a pile of animals in the middle of the portal field at Ravenswood.

"Are you okay" Tasha rushed toward them, magic meter in hand.

"Look what I found!" Ozzie crowed, holding up his prize.

Bathed in the light of the flashing green crystal, quiffles, brimbees, and wommels turned on Ozzie with a strange glint in their eyes.

"Don't all thank me at once."

Like a wild pack, the magical animals charged, flattening the ferret.

"GAH!"

Tasha pointed her magic meter into the melee. "These readings are off the charts! That crystal is driving the animals wild."

Ozzie slipped away from the pile, only to be tackled by Lyra.

"Where's Kara?" the cat roared furiously.

"Ozzie, stop it!" Tasha cried.

The ferret ran in circles, Lyra and the animals on his heels. "Helllllllp!"

"The crystal, make it stop!" Tasha dodged a flying quiffle. "It's making everyone crazy!"

Ozzie spun around, brandishing the jewel. "Back off!"

With a flash, the crystal's magic dimmed under his control.

Lyra shook her head, confused. *"What happened?"*

Ozzie kicked at her. "You tried to eat me!"

"Sorry."

"Amazing!" Tasha scanned Ozzie and the power crystal. "The power crystal's dark magic didn't affect your ferret stone at all."

"Yeah, thanks for the help," Ozzie said sarcastically.

In a flurry of twigs, Tweek materialized with a crunch. "I'm ba-AAK!"

The Experimental Fairimental's quartz eyes bugged out and twirled as the power crystal enveloped him in murky light.

"Hold yourself together, twigman." Ozzie turned the jewel away from the E.F.

"I don't believe it!" Tasha gasped, wide eyes glued to her screen.

The group circled Tasha.

"What's happening?" Lorren asked.

"The Spider Witch has made her move. She's added the Gates of Avalon to her web," Tasha whispered.

Glowing green lines reached out greedily from the Spider Witch's lair in the Fairy Realms, snaking tendrils across the web and locking in the final power crystal, the Heart of Avalon. Everyone stared at the image, shocked.

"There it is! The Gates of Avalon!" Rasha said, stunned.

"We *have* to get to there," Tasha exclaimed. "Now!"

"We're missing a crystal!" Tweek fretted.

"Actually, we're not. Kara made one," Lorren said icily.

"Where? How? Who?" Tweek spluttered.

"What's that?" Ozzie pointed to a blinking light moving across the web.

Tasha's face went pale. "Emily's jewel. But it's totally dark." She flipped a switch. Two other dark spots appeared on the map of the web. "Adriane and Kara. Their readings have gone dark as well."

"Wait," Ozzie said. "You said Kara's crystal was acting funny. Adriane's too. Now Emily has one in the center of the witch's web. And now this one," he held his crystal tight. "They're all bonding with dark crystals."

"I knew Kara was acting weird!" Lorren exclaimed.

"We have to get to the mages!" Tasha cried.

"Let's go!" Tweek yelled.

"Get us to Adriane!" the quiffles shouted.

"Get me to Kara!" Lyra howled.

The ferret pulled Lyra aside as the group rushed to open the Ravenswood portal.

"Lyra, I've got a bad feeling about this. We don't know how the dark crystals are affecting the mages." The cat held her head close to Ozzie as he whispered. "What's going to happen when we put the power crystals all together? We can't risk bringing everyone into something really dangerous."

Lyra glanced at Tasha, Lorren, Tweek, and the animals.

"Okay," Tweek announced. "I've sequenced a series of portals we can jump through, the final one will lead to Emily."

Suddenly, the Ravenswood portal swirled open, casting a weird, diffused glow over the field. The protective dreamcatcher hung in its center, the Spider Witch's sickly green magic slithering over its strands.

"Let's go!" The entire group charged, all preparing to jump into the Ravenswood portal.

With a roar, Lyra leaped in their path.

"What are you doing?" Lorren tried to step around her. "Let us through!"

Lyra firmly stood her ground.

"Listen up!" Ozzie ordered. "We know the witch has control of the web." The ferret scratched his chin thoughtfully. "What we don't know is, well, everything else."

The group ignored him, surging forward.

"Wait!" Ozzie implored his friends. "I grew up on Aldenmor and I've traveled all over the web, but the only home I've ever had is Ravenswood. No matter what happens to the rest of us, I'm counting on you to protect our home."

The last traces of anger and confusion left his friends' faces.

"You too, Lorren. We need you here."

Slowly, the goblin prince bowed. "Good luck, Sir Ozymandias."

Nodding in silent thanks, the ferret leaped onto Lyra's back.

With a final glance at their friends, Lyra and Ozzie jumped through the portal, leaving Ravenswood behind.

23

*J*OYOUS ROARS AND licks of flame flashed off the majestic mountains. In the hidden valley below, a raucous dragon celebration was underway. Living, breathing dragons of countless myths, their hides midnight blue, iridescent bronze, and every color in between—all crowded around Drake and Gwyx, congratulating the returning heroes, two of their own.

His long snout raised to the air, the massive High Wyvern spread his battle-scarred green wings and belched fire into the skies.

The others quieted immediately as their leader spoke. *"This is a glorious day for Dragon Home! Gwylrrtrwrx has returned victorious from his quest to slay the shadow dragon.*

And he has brought a long lost red crystal dragon brother with him."

Several dragons draped their wings around Gywx, jockeying for a position close to the great warrior. A pretty turquoise female batted her eyes and snorted a flirtatious puff of steam. Gwyx soaked it all in, his pointy teeth bared in a wide grin.

Drake stood beside him, snorting in pleasure to finally be in Dragon Home.

"Brother Gwylrrtrwrx," the High Wyvern continued. *"For your bravery and service to the dragons and all of Dragon Home, you shall no longer be known as Runs-with-Tail."*

"Finally!" Gwyx practically drooled dragon slobber.

"From this day forth, your new warrior name is Shadow Slayer."

"That is the meanest, baddest name ever bestowed upon a dragon!" Gwyx pumped his front paw in the air. *"I accept."*

His friends roared with approval, ready to party.

"Pass the firefloggin!" a blue-coated dragon bellowed.

"The brew you can spew," chortled his green companion.

The two dragons roared with laughter and crashed their chests together in a dragon toast.

"Do the Dragon Stomp!" A huge, purple dragon stomped his feet. Dozens of others joined in, shaking the ground so hard rocks tumbled down the mountains.

"Welcome to Dragon Home, Drake." A silver dragon sidled up to Drake, who responded by sniffing at his magic. *"You are the first outsider ever to set foot in this secret valley."*

"There is more dragon magic here than I ever imagined," Drake replied, excited to be among other dragons for the first time in his life.

Gwyx pulled Drake back to his side. *"I'd trust this dragon with my left wing. It's like we were hatched from the same egg!"*

Six young dragons ran up to the newly christened Shadow Slayer, pulling at his wings.

"Tell us how you slew the monster," a golden youngling asked, his eyes wide in awe. Others echoed, *"Yes, tell us everything, Shadow Slayer."*

"The shadow creature was so afraid of me that it died of fright rather than do battle," Gwyx boasted.

The dragons roared with laughter. The younglings hung on every word.

"The monster was huge. Biggest and fastest dragon I've ever seen! But I was faster." Gwyx spun quickly, dramatizing the moves he had supposedly made in the fight. *"It attacked with brutal strength, but I took the beast down with a fatal blow."*

He glanced at Drake, but the red dragon was wandering through the party, intently studying the others.

"Drake helped me, of course. It is a miracle I have brought him to our secret home before any humans could find him. He would have become a slave instead of a hero."

The young dragons snorted smoke. *"Yeah, foul humans."*

Gwyx ran over to Drake and pulled him away from the High Wyvern. *"Over here, Brother Drake. Let us revel in my, I mean, our, victory. This is the best moment of my life!"*

Pop!

A strange, very undragon-like sound interrupted the celebration.

"Hey, a party!" In a cloud of pink twinkles, Kara materialized.

The dragons gaped in disbelief at the creature that had just appeared in the center of their festivities.

"What's that?" A youngling snuffled up to Kara, his snout steaming.

"Hey, watch the hair," she admonished him.

Fireballs exploded over her head, courtesy of dozens of stunned dragons roaring in fury.

"A human!" A cobalt-blue dragon was furious.

"This is outrageous!" a lime-green one thundered.

"Ew, I touched it!" The golden youngling jumped away, disgusted.

Dozens of dragon warriors charged at Kara, flames shooting from their angry snouts. The sight of them would have scared the living daylights out of anyone. Not the blazing star.

Shimmering magic flew from Kara's fingers, meeting dragon fire with elemental fire. Dragon fire bounced right back at the massive warriors.

"What's with you guys?" the blazing star demanded

with a toss of her golden tresses. "I just got styled at the Fashion Realm."

"The human is going to take our magic!" a furious dragon hollered.

"No, I'm not—well, except his." Kara waved happily at her friend. "Hi Drake!"

Every dragon eye turned to Gwyx and Drake.

The High Wyvern towered above them. *"What false-hood have you told us? Instead of killing our enemies, you have brought one right into our home! You betrayed us!"*

Gwyx leaped away from Drake, his wings fluttering nervously. *"Don't blame me. I hardly know the guy."*

"No human has ever found Dragon Home," the leader bellowed. *"You brought her here!"*

"Oh, chill out. I'm not staying." Kara tapped her foot impatiently. "Let's go Drake, we have to get to the Gates of Avalon."

"Drake!" the High Wyvern thundered. *"Are you with us or the human?"*

Drake eyed Kara suspiciously. *"I never saw this human before!"*

Kara rolled her eyes. "Don't be silly, Drake." She turned to the elder dragons "He's a little shy. Drake is with me. He's bonded to Adriane—"

Drake stepped away from the blazing star. *"No self-respecting dragon would ever bond with a human!"*

Pop! Another strange sound echoed through the valley.

The purple dragonfly Barney suddenly appeared on Kara's shoulder. "Hi."

The mini took one look at the army of giant, angry dragons and freaked.

"Oh no, you don't." Kara held Barney up to her ear.

Tasha's worried voice blasted from Barney's belly. "Princess, are you there?"

"'Sup?" Kara asked.

The dragons stared in disbelief at the little, purple d-fly.

"Do you mind, this is private," Kara told the astonished dragons.

"Lorren said you made a crystal," Tasha said.

Kara beamed. "Cool, huh? I got this really rad shell and—"

"Where are you?" Tasha asked.

"I'm at Dragon Home with Drake." Kara slid away from the angry throng.

"Where's Adriane?"

"How should I know?" Kara snapped.

"Wait, what are you doing with Drake?"

"I need his magic to finish the power crystal."

"One dragon for a whole power crystal?" Tasha seemed surprised.

"It's arcane magic, very scientific," the blazing star explained.

"Kara, that is really dangerous stuff."

"Don't worry. Tell the others to forget The Garden and get to the island, pronto."

"But what about the crystals at the jewel vault?" Tasha asked.

"I'll take care of it. Gotta go. I got a hundred dragons staring at me."

Barney vanished in a burst of bubbles the instant Kara let go.

She shrugged. "Drake, come on, you're throwing me way off schedule here," she said impatiently.

"I found my home and I'm not leaving," Drake insisted.

"Yes you are," the High Wyvern roared. *"No one who leads a human to our secret home can stay."*

His wrathful glare settled on Gwyx. *"You have endangered us all."*

"It was all his fault." Gwyx cowered, pointing both wings at Drake.

"You are hereby banished from Dragon Home!" the leader declared with a stomp of his foot.

"When can I come back?"

"Never!"

Gwyx hung his head. *"Can I keep my name?"*

"No!"

The shamed black dragon glared at Drake and Kara. *"I'll get you for this! You haven't seen the last of me!"*

The red dragon shuffled from foot to foot. *"I must stay and stomp with my brothers and sisters!"*

"Quit acting so weird, we're going to find Avalon," Kara's voice was all no-nonsense. "What's the matter with you?"

Drake backed away. *"I… uh…"*

"Forget it, I don't have time to argue." Kara took the wishing crystal from her jacket pocket and pointed it at Drake. "Drake, I wish you would come with me to the Gates of Avalon."

In a sparkling cloud, blazing star and dragon disappeared.

24

O N A W I D E plateau halfway up the snow covered
slopes of Mt. Hope, the misty shape of a girl knelt
in the center of her bother and sister wolves. The pack
circled her, nearly three hundred strong. Raising their
heads to the sunset skies, their wolfsong rang through the
thick forests of Packhome. Lone wolves no longer, each
packmate joined with every other in the haunting cry.

The power crystal embedded in Adriane's chest
vibrated with the mighty sound. The warrior stiffened,
struggling to free herself from the crystal's hold and
return to solid form. Connected to the strength of every
wolf, she longed to run with the pack, to feel her paws
padding over wet grass, the infinite wonder of the forest
surrounding her.

The wolf song's melody rose and fell like the timeless cycle of the moons. Adriane swayed to the howling chorus. She knew the pack's trail led toward an uncertain future, yet the one thing that would stay constant, forever sure, was the familiar, comforting scent of the pack. She was at the center of a never-ending circle, perfect and whole, always there to lead her home.

Adriane opened her eyes. She lifted her arms and exhaled slowly. Her wolf stone gleamed on her solid wrist. She quickly felt her legs, then rose to her feet, testing the weight of her boots against the forest floor. With the combined strength of the pack's magic, she was finally in human form again.

Hundreds of bright wolf eyes focused on her, the spell of the wolf song echoing into the evening skies. With a yelp, Adriane ran toward Dreamer and hugged him tight, burying her face in his warm black fur.

"It is good to see you again, packmate." Dreamer licked her face.

"Good to be seen." Adriane laughed.

"Welcome back, wolf sister," a female wolf greeted her.

Adriane grinned at the magnificent gold and white wolf, the alpha female of the pack.

"Dawnrunner!" Adriane hugged the wolf, delighting in her cinnamon-sweet fur.

"Why must you always stick your nose into trouble?" another wolf growled at her.

For a second, Adriane completely forgot her wolf

etiquette and rushed to throw her arms around the packleader. She stopped herself at the last moment and kneeled before the huge black mistwolf. "Moonshadow, you honor me," she said with reverence.

The packleader moved closer, until he was nose-to-nose with the warrior. *"You are wolf sister to the pack. But you bring foul magic to Packhome."*

"Packleader, I would never willingly bring danger to the pack, but danger has followed my trail."

Several wolves warily sniffed the power crystal, which now lay in the center of the wolf circle shimmering with an unearthly glow.

Dawnrunner growled and shoved her mate aside. *"Can you not see our sister has hunted well?"*

"What she has brought is made of shadow," a brown and silver wolf declared. *"Powerful dark magic."*

"And you bonded with this crystal," Moonshadow growled.

"It is a power crystal of Avalon." Adriane bowed her head in submission to the great wolf. "If the pack hadn't helped me, I would have been trapped by its dark magic."

Moonshadow's deep golden eyes studied hers. *"Do not be deceived, warrior. You have been touched by darkness in your most vulnerable form. The wolf runs strong inside you, but the shadow now lies waiting, fearsome in its power."*

Adriane flinched. Even as the packleader spoke, she could feel the darkness like night in her veins.

"She and Dreamer run to save our world." Dawnrunner ignored her mate's grumbling. *"You were right to come, sister."*

Brrrrring. The familiar sound of a dragonfly rang out.

"Welcome back, Fred," Adriane said as the blue d-fly hugged her neck, his eyes whirling in relief.

"Adriane?" Tasha's voice came through Fred's belly. "Are you all right?"

"Yes. Did you find Emily?" Adriane suddenly remembered her missing friend.

"We think she's already at the island or on her way."

"And Kara?" the warrior asked coldly.

"I just talked to her. She made a replacement crystal."

"She did?" Adriane couldn't hide her surprise. How could Kara have accomplished in a few hours something Tasha couldn't do after months of research?

Tasha hesitated. "And she's taking Drake to the Gates of Avalon."

"What? Why in the world would she need Drake?"

"She needs his magic for the crystal."

Anger flared through Adriane, making her wolf stone flash dark gray. What did Kara think she was doing? The last time she took magic, she couldn't control herself. And now she was expecting Drake's magic to finish something as huge as a power crystal?

"Tasha, how could Kara make a power crystal so fast?"

"She's using strong magic." The goblin sorceress gulped.

Adriane glowered, her suspicions confirmed. "Dark magic, you mean."

"Um, I suppose so," Tasha answered in a tiny voice.

Adriane could sense the goblin teen was at her wit's end. She had to respect that Tasha would never say anything bad about Kara. But Adriane could read between the lines. Even Tasha didn't trust Kara now.

"Adriane, she said she was going to get the crystals from the vault to the island, too."

"This is not good."

"Ozzie found the last crystal and left for the gates to find Emily. That leaves you."

"I have my crystal," Adriane told Tasha. "I can take the Spirit Trail to the Gates of Avalon. I've done it before."

"You've got to hurry. I'm really worried…"

Tasha didn't have to finish her thought.

Adriane was on it. "I'm on my way."

The warrior broke the connection, worry clouding her dark eyes.

"Speak with us, warrior," Dawnrunner urged.

Adriane gazed at the pack she loved. Her heart filled with pride as she looked upon each of her brothers and sisters. Turning to Moonshadow, she spoke bluntly, warrior to warrior.

"I must leave to complete my quest. The Spider Witch is weaving her web and I suspect my power crystal isn't the only one filled with dark magic. I don't know what will happen when we open the Gates of Avalon. I ask you to stand ready to protect Aldenmor, and if necessary, the web itself."

Moonshadow faced Adriane, wolf eyes gleaming. *"I have made a pledge to the Fairimentals to protect Aldenmor."* The packleader glanced at Dawnrunner. *"I have more reason than ever to protect the pack."*

"I carry his pups." Dawnrunner smiled a wolfish grin.

Adriane hugged Dawnrunner again, eyes damp with joy for her sister. "My heart sings for you."

Moonshadow faced the warrior. *"Do not let fear overpower you, warrior. You must remain strong."*

"I will." The warrior was more determined than ever to keep the pack safe for all the mistwolves who had yet to run.

Adriane clenched her fists as Kara flashed in her mind. When Kara lashed out to take Zach's magic, the Dark Sorceress had been there, controlling the water Fairimental, Marina. Adriane knew the Dark Sorceress had given up too easily after their battle on Aldenmor.

If controlling Marina and the dragon eggs had been her true objective, she would not simply have vanished.

Was there something more to the sorceress's plans? Adriane had a terrible feeling she knew what it was. What if the sorceress turned one of the mages? And who else would the Dark Sorceress choose but Kara? It was a serious accusation, but Kara had betrayed the mages before, and her relation to the Dark Sorceress made her more vulnerable to the evil woman's attacks.

It all seemed clear now—Adriane knew what she had to do to keep her pack safe.

"We will wait for your signal, warrior," Moonshadow said.

"May you run strong, packmates," Dawnrunner called to Adriane and Dreamer.

The warrior's senses tingled as the wolf pack raised their heads as one, sending the wolfsong into the star-streaked sky. The voices of a thousand mistwolves answered, their paws thundering over Packhome as they came to greet her. Through the trees, a glittering blue pathway swirled open, beckoning Adriane and Dreamer onto the ancient trail to Avalon.

25

*T*HE DARK SORCERESS stood on her balcony, overlooking the courtyard behind her lair. The night skies glittered with a thousand stars. Eyes closed, she tasted the air, sensing the shift in the magic. "Can you feel it?"

Henry Gardner stood beside her, pale and gaunt. The wizard had been drained to his limit. "We're too late."

The sorceress inhaled deeply, as if the new web gave her strength. "There was no way the old web could have survived. I realized that when I saw the tapestry for Silvan's new design. So perfect in every detail. That's when I decided to help the mages."

"You knew that once she wove enough of her web, the Gates of Avalon would be revealed." Gardener watched as, below, the sorceress's minions moved hundreds of cages into the courtyard. Shrieks and howls of the shadow creatures filled the night. They too could feel the shifting web and were hungry for its magic.

"That's why you collected the shadow creatures," he continued, a tinge of admiration in his voice. "I am impressed by your foresight."

"My creatures will take the magic from her web. So you see, dear friend, in the end, I will have it all. The power crystals, the magic, the new web, even Avalon."

Her blood-red lips curved. "It will be quite amusing to devise a prison for the witch. Perhaps I'll weave her into one of those horrible cocoons she seems to enjoy so much."

She caught the faraway look in Gardener's eyes.

"Oh, come now, Henry. Why so glum? From the ashes of our failure, I shall rise like a phoenix ascending!"

"I only wish I could have gotten to know the mages better," Gardener said sadly.

Her animal eyes caught a fleeting glimpse of the past, at the friends she once loved. "You did the best you could, Henry. You tried to find the crystals for them. But the mages are going to complete their quest, even without your help. Rest assured, dear Henry. I will carry on your work. The dark mage will be an able apprentice."

Gardener's mouth twitched in a smile. "They are extraordinary girls. They may surprise you."

The sorceress studied him closely. "I doubt it. The blazing star is on her way to Avalon. I knew the dark fairy would help her."

"Since when do you trust dark fairies?"

"Trust? This is business. Where do you think I acquired these marvelous creatures?"

The sorceress circled the wizard like a cat. "Henry, dear, I fear our time together is at an end. I have enjoyed your company, but I must take what magic you have left."

Gardner nodded. He knew exactly what happened when the Dark Sorceress no longer had need of someone.

"I know you're as curious as I am to learn what lies behind the gates." She paused to look in his eyes. "I don't suppose you want to just *give* me your magic. For old time's sake?"

His expression hardened.

She sighed. "Yes, I thought as much."

The shadow creatures shifted along Gardener's back, sinking tendrils deep into his flesh.

"You may live long enough to see me return and welcome the blazing star." She stroked the dark smudges beneath his shirt. "But I doubt you'll recognize me."

Gardener cried out, collapsing as she extracted strands of glimmering energy.

The magic flew from her fingertips. Below, the cages cracked opened.

Black robes billowing behind her, the sorceress waved her hands and the shadow creatures took flight. The demons coursed across the sky in a wave of blackness as the Dark Sorceress's animal eyes settled on Henry Gardner for the last time. "Goodbye, old friend."

26

MIST ROSE FROM the glittering mosaic floor, lazily drifting over the ancient ring. Giant stone pillars surrounded the pattern of interlocking stones, their towering surfaces sparkling with colorful gems. In the distance, palms swayed in the breeze, but nothing in the outside world seemed to affect this place. The tiles were pristine, ageless, untouched by sand, undamaged by wind and sun. In the center of the ring, a heart-shaped crystal—the Heart of Avalon—floated, waiting, for this was the entrance to Avalon.

Simultaneously, two flashes of light flared on opposite sides of the ring. On one side, Adriane and Dreamer appeared back-to-back, alert for danger. On the other side, Kara and Drake materialized.

A power crystal shone in the palm of each mage's hand. The warrior's, dark and mysterious as the night. The blazing star's, bright and brilliant as the midday sun. The mages eyed one another warily, crystals sparking with power waiting to be unleashed.

"*Help!*" Drake cried, lumbering toward Adriane. "*She's going to take my magic!*"

With a wave of her hand, Kara stopped him, trapping the red dragon in a gleaming force field.

"Let him go," the warrior snarled.

The blazing star, confident as always, tossed her golden locks over her shoulder. "No can do. He's going to help me finish my power crystal."

Adriane took a step forward. "Doesn't look like he wants to help you."

"We need a replacement crystal," Kara argued.

"Because you destroyed one." Adriane's wolf stone flashed darkly upon her wrist.

"Thank goodness I have you to remind me like every five seconds," Kara sneered.

Adriane's body stiffened. "Time and time again, you've proven you can't control your magic. You care about one thing and one thing only: Miss Kara 'best-mage-on-the-planet' Davies."

"That's rich, coming from the lone wolf," Kara shot back.

"This time you've gone too far." Adriane pointed at the dazzling power crystal in Kara's hand. "You're using a dark crystal."

"It hasn't affected me. I'm totally fine," Kara retorted.

"Then where's Lyra?"

Kara stopped short. A spark of red flared from the unicorn jewel on her necklace.

Adriane continued. "How can you possibly stand there and tell me you're fine when who knows what you did with your own bonded?"

"You did the same thing!" Kara was furious. "You left Drake!"

"I had no choice. At the time, the jewel had me trapped."

"Oh, you mean that dark crystal?" She pointed at Adriane's shadow crystal. "You are such a hypocrite!"

Adriane's hand twitched, sending a silent signal to Dreamer. The mistwolf moved slowly toward Kara.

The blazing star's fingers closed tightly around the wishing crystal. "When *you* use a power crystal, it's fine 'cause you're Adriane, the 'do-everything-right-all-the-time' warrior. But when *I* use one, I must be evil. After all this time, you still don't trust me."

"Give me a reason to trust you." Adriane took another step forward, wolf stone raised. "Let Drake go."

Kara stepped back, forcing Drake to follow. "We're here to put the jewels in place," she said calmly. "*All* the jewels."

Warrior and blazing star circled the ring. Fueled by the power crystals, wolf stone and unicorn jewel pulsated with light.

"What did you do with the crystals from the vault?" Adriane demanded.

"Oh, right." Kara tapped her chin and held up the wishing crystal. "You know, I really *wish* those power crystals were here."

Instantly, three power crystals sparkled into sight, floating in the center of the ring. Three dazzling jewels retrieved by the mages early on in their quest, kept safe until all nine could be gathered and used to open the Gates of Avalon.

"Well, look at that," Kara gloated. "Cool, huh?"

Adriane stepped back. "How did you do that?"

"I have the perfect crystal to make all my dreams come true. A wishing crystal." Kara's grin was wide, and triumphant.

"That's ridiculous."

"Oh, really? What's yours?"

"A shadow crystal." Adriane raised the dark jewel.

"Ooooo, I'm shaking in my Manolos."

"Oh yeah?" Adriane taunted. "Try it on for size."

Instantly, a bolt fired from the shadow crystal, covering Kara in shimmering purple smoke. With a *pop*, the blazing star vanished.

"Hey!" Kara's voice called from where she had been standing. "Where'd I go?"

"Probably the mall, as usual," Adriane smirked.

"I wish to come back," Kara exclaimed forcefully.

Kara popped back wearing an entirely new outfit. She

smoothed her designer jeans and pink top. "Ah. Much more suitable for kicking your butt."

"You'll have to do better than that if you want to take over the web."

Kara thought for a moment. "I wish I had a horrible beast to fight Adriane!"

A geyser of smoke and fire shot from the ground. Kara leaped away as molten hands reached from the earth, heaving up a hulking body of solid stone.

"Rock on!" Kara cheered.

"Hi, everyone." In a flash of light, Ozzie and Lyra magically joined the mages. "We're he—GaH!

Ozzie scrambled out of the way as the stone creature tore from the ground and charged Adriane, its huge feet crunching the ancient tiles.

Adriane was not intimidated. She whipped a cord of silver wolf fire around the thing's big feet and pulled hard. The monster toppled over in a spray of flying rocks and dirt.

"Well, that's a fine how do you do!" Ozzie huffed, arms crossed over his ferret chest.

Lyra's eyes flickered between her bonded and the warrior. *"Kara, what are you doing?"*

"What does it look like I'm doing?"

"How should I know, you wished me away!" the cat snarled.

"That was the lamest zombie I've ever seen!" Adriane exulted in her easy take-down.

"Shows what you know. It was a golem."

"Hey," Ozzie called out, refusing to be ignored. "Look what I found."

He raised his power crystal. In a blaze of light, the crystal flew from his hands, whooshing into the center of the ring with the other jewels.

"It's one of those in there." Ozzie gulped as black smoke seeped from his crystal, bleeding dark magic into the four pure crystals. "Uh oh."

Lyra growled at Adriane and Kara's jewels. *"Those are dark crystals. Can't you feel it?"*

"Yeah, and maybe you're a dark mage!" Kara challenged Adriane.

"I am not. You are!"

"Where's Emily?" Ozzie interrupted their bickering.

Kara ignored the ferret and kept needling her ex-friend. "You're the one who came in and started accusing me when I didn't do anything."

"Typical," Adriane groused, "you never admit you're wrong."

"Maybe because you think I do *everything* wrong!"

"You got that right."

"Enough!" Ozzie shouted, paws over his ears. "Listen to me! These jewels are driving both of you crazy with dark magic. I just saw it happen to the animals back at Ravenswood. We don't know what kind of magic we're going to set loose from Avalon, but I'm pretty sure it's not good. So just calm down."

"I released magic from the crystals before and it was good," Kara reasoned. "I can do it again."

"That was before you turned dark," Adriane countered.

"And you turned into a loser. Oh wait, you already were a loser."

"Keep it together," Ozzie pleaded. "We're still missing Emily and her jewel. Then we'll have all nine."

"Assuming Kara's new one works," Adriane muttered.

Lyra growled at Kara. "*Don't ever wish me away again!*"

"What is the big deal? You wouldn't let me make the replacement crystal so I sent you home."

"Put that wishing crystal with the others," Adriane ordered.

"I need it to finish this one." Kara reached into her pocket and withdrew the shell she and Logan had made.

"You're just trying to keep it for yourself!" Adriane accused.

"Here we are at the Gates of Avalon, and you two are fighting like five-year-olds. Just finish your crystal and let's get on with it!" Ozzie ordered Kara.

"I can't do it until Emily gets here with hers."

"What did you do, wish her away, too?" Adriane snapped.

"I'm right here."

Emily stood on the opposite side of the ring, red power crystal gleaming in her hands.

Ozzie charged over, skidding to a stop at the healer's feet.

"Emily, are you okay?" He studied his friend carefully.

"I … don't know," she said sluggishly. "I need to heal the web."

"Emily!" Adriane called out. "Kara won't give up her crystal."

"Emily, tell Adriane to put hers in first!" Kara commanded.

"Please don't fight," the healer said in a strangely quiet voice. "We don't have much time."

The healer released her crystal. It floated into the center of the ring with the others. Now there were six: the Heart of Avalon, three from The Garden's vault, one from Emily, and one from Ozzie. Power radiated from the jewels, streaking the sky with deep purple. The air felt heavy as the magic built.

"What do we do?" Ozzie asked anxiously, his ferret face creased with worry. "These crystals are all dark."

"We have to open the Gates of Avalon," Emily whispered. "Adriane, let go of your power crystal."

"Not until she does." The warrior glared at Kara.

"Do as she says!" Ozzie ordered. Something was very wrong with Emily. It seemed as if she were struggling against a powerful force, something other than the dark crystals.

"We have one chance to fix everything." Emily's limp curls hung in her face. "We can do it together, but I need all of you. Now."

"Emily, we're here for you," Ozzie said soothingly. "Everything's going to be okay."

Adriane glowered at Kara. "I'm warning you, Kara, if you hurt Drake..."

Reluctantly, the warrior released her crystal into the ring. Purple shadow magic joined the swirling lights of the other crystals. Now there were seven.

Angry clouds roiled overhead, reflected by the eerily glowing crystals.

"Kara, hurry," Emily pleaded.

"Do it, Kara!" Ozzie cried.

Kara held up the shell of the power crystal she'd created with Logan. "Drake, give me your magic."

"*No,*" the dragon refused.

Exasperated, Kara yelled, "We have to open the gates, come on!"

"He must have a good reason for refusing you," the warrior growled, her body tense.

"If he doesn't give it to me, then I'll have to take it." Kara was obstinate.

"Just like you stole Zach's?" Silver fire sparked from Adriane's wrist.

"I made another power crystal, figured everything out, and you're *still* not satisfied."

"And just how are you supposed to get Drake's magic in there?" Adriane challenged.

That was a good question. Kara had never thought that far ahead. "Geez, I wish I knew."

All the air seemed to drain from the ring. For a split second, no one could breathe.

Then the warrior was in a fighting stance, magic crackling around her like lightning. Her eyes burned with fury. "I *knew* it."

Ozzie leaped back, gaping at Kara.

Lyra and Dreamer snarled, turning on the blazing star.

Confused, Kara followed their gaze. The crystal she and Logan had made had transformed into a gleaming black dagger.

"How did that happen?" Kara stuttered, horrified.

"Get away from him." Adriane hissed, rings of silver fire swirling dangerously from her raised fists.

Kara looked at the dagger, then at Drake. The dragon's eyes locked on hers, deep and menacing. Ice clamped around her heart like a vise as fear lanced up her spine. She needed powerful magic to finish the final power crystal. Everything she wanted was almost hers. Thanks to the wishing jewel, she finally understood what she had to do.

She raised the dagger, magic glinting along the curved blade.

"You wouldn't kill an innocent dragon, would you?" Drake asked.

Kara looked him straight in the eyes. "No, I wouldn't."

In a single swift motion, the blazing star plunged the dagger deep into the dragon's heart.

Drake collapsed, writhing as black smoke poured from his wound.

Howling, Adriane attacked Kara with the full force of her magic.

Kara flew backwards, careening across the floor, crashing hard into a stone pillar. Arms flailing, she desperately tried to raise a protective shield as wolf fire exploded around her.

Lyra charged Adriane, teeth bared, roaring in rage.

"Lyra!" Kara screamed, struggling to her feet. "No!

Dreamer lunged at the cat, his sharp teeth sinking into Lyra's neck, ripping her away from the warrior. Lyra thrashed and yowled as blood splattered her orange fur.

Diamond fire blasted from Kara's outstretched hands and smashed into the mistwolf.

The mages were locked in battle, just like so many times before.

"Stop it!" Ozzie screamed as Adriane steadily advanced on Kara, firing bolt after bolt of wolf fire.

"Adriane, you don't understand!" Kara's shield buckled. Even her blazing star magic could not withstand the righteous wrath of the warrior.

The dagger slipped from Drake's chest, and the ground beneath them shook.

"Something's happening!" Ozzie cried.

Wind howled across the ancient ring. The pillars began to glow as the last two crystals rose from the ground beside Drake.

"It worked." Kara's wide eyes watched her two crystals floating to join the others.

The moment they had all been working so hard for, risking their lives for, was upon them—the culmination of the prophecy, the completion of their quest.

But it was not what any of them had envisioned.

Nine power crystals spun in a blaze of magic, blurring red, orange, green, purple, blue, and silver. The colors twisted, melting into deep, pulsing black. Where nine crystals had floated, now there was only one. One power crystal. One key.

A single prism of light shot from the key, and then another, and another, until nine beams formed a perfect circle, hovering above the ancient floor. It was not like any portal the mages had ever seen. The surface was covered in facets of moving light, like a jewel.

Oblivious to everything, Adriane and Kara tumbled on the ground, literally at each other's throats.

"Stop it! Stop it!" Ozzie frantically ran around the two mages. "Can't you see what's happening?"

Emily slowly advanced toward the portal as tendrils of mist reached for her like fingers.

Lyra arched her back and hissed. Dreamer began snapping at the air.

Like a dam bursting open, magic surged through the gateway engulfing Emily in a maelstrom of dark power. Silken strands, glistening like mirrors, looped and swirled around her. She called Indi, the heart of her magic, but her paladin had been turned, his twisted magic burning at her senses. She couldn't see the ring or her friends any more.

"Adriane, Kara," Emily tried to call out, but her voice was so weak. She knew no one heard. Bright patterns and shapes rocketed through her mind until she could see nothing but chaotic swirls of magic. She tried again to speak, but only managed a hoarse whisper. "Help me."

Suddenly, in the sea of kaleidoscopic colors, one bright orange glow seemed to separate from the blur. She grabbed for it like a lifeline.

Ozzie rushed toward his friend. "Emily, hold on!"

"Ozzie," she cried, reaching blindly for him. "I can't see you!"

"I'm right here."

Emily tried to explain. "I have to get this magic onto the Spider Witch's web."

Ozzie felt a chill go up his spine. Had he heard her correctly? Emily was going to help the Spider Witch?

Ozzie planted himself in front of Emily, ferret stone blazing. There was no way he would let his friend fall to the witch.

Colors flashed and warped in Emily's mind as she grabbed Ozzie's magic. "Don't leave me, I'm so scared."

"I'll never leave you." Ozzie entwined his magic with hers. He would never let go. "You take care of me. I take care of you."

Time and again, the brave ferret had saved Emily through the power of his friendship. And no matter how bad he felt about himself, about his life as a ferret, she would always find his golden aura and make it sparkle.

But this time it was Ozzie who saw Emily's aura. Avalon's magic was so powerful, she had begun to shimmer, her true colors visible. A beautiful rainbow cascaded around her like summer rain. But it was being washed away as darkness swirled over her eyes.

"Emily," the ferret rasped as the healer locked onto his stone. Still Ozzie stood strong, refusing to let Emily go, even as he knew his friend was slipping away.

All at once Emily saw everything with crystal clarity. The Spider Witch's web lay before her. It was beautiful, perfect, each newly formed strand carefully laid in place. All it needed was magic.

With a final pull, she ripped the last shreds of her best friend's magic away from him.

Everything was surreal, as if happening in slow motion, as Ozzie's jewel exploded.

The weaver raised her rainbow jewel to the skies and summoned the dark creatures who would spread Avalon's magic.

Across the ring, Adriane and Kara still struggled, oblivious to the danger, and to Emily.

"Adriane, stop it!" Kara screamed. "The portal's open!"

"You killed him!" Adriane cried.

"Oh no! Who died?"

The warrior and the blazing star froze as Drake sat up, staring at them both with worried golden eyes.

Adriane could barely speak. "Drake, you're alive?"

"Yes, Mama, I'm fine."

Adriane turned to Kara, stunned. "I don't understand."

Kara gasped for breath. "There was a shadow creature inside him, I tried to tell you! I used *its* magic to finish the crystal, not Drake's."

"The shadow dragon! Why didn't you say something?"

"I didn't know for sure until the last minute. You really think I would have killed Drake?"

The sound of hooves suddenly filled the air as hundreds of unicorns surrounded the ring, stomping and snorting.

"The unicorns!" Adriane exclaimed.

Kara's face lit up. Then she saw the red magic swirling from their horns. "Wait... something's wrong."

Portals exploded open in blinding flares. Adriane and Kara shielded their eyes from the intense light as, one by one, the unicorns leaped, trailing the magic of Avalon behind them.

Frantically, Emily wove, feeding dark magic to the unicorns.

At her feet, Ozzie's body lay still on the cold ground.

"Ozzie?" Adriane called out nervously.

"Emily, what happened?" Kara was almost afraid to find out.

Ignoring them, the healer stood over the small, furry figure, her fingers glowing red.

The sound of clapping echoed across the ring

"Bravo." A tall, cloaked figure stood behind them. The Dark Sorceress smiled. Adriane and Kara leaped to their feet, bondeds by their side. Silver and diamond white magic shot from their jewels, smashing into their enemy. But the magic failed to touch her.

Ghastly creatures burst from thin air, wings, claws, and teeth glinting with malice. The shadow creatures latched onto the mages' magic, absorbing it with voracious hunger. Kara and Adriane were pulled to their knees as they tried to control their jewels. Dreamer, Lyra, and Drake roared in pain.

"Adriane, stop!" Kara cried. "They'll take all our magic!"

With a scream, Adriane yanked her magic free. She scrambled to her packmate, soothing him as Kara hugged Lyra.

"The three mages. The grand hope of the Fairimentals." The sorceress walked toward the Gates of Avalon. "The Prophecy of Three has come to pass. It always ends with one mage turning dark and betraying the others. It has happened over and over again. You know why? Because Avalon is dark, it has always been dark. And the only *real* chosen ones are the dark mages."

The sorceress pinned Kara with her animal eyes. "Kara, join me now." She extended a pale hand. "Become the blazing star you were meant to be."

Kara glanced at Adriane. The warrior watched her warily. Emily stood over Ozzie, as if she were trying to heal him.

"I'm not going anywhere with you," Kara said firmly. She walked over and stood next to Adriane. "I'm staying where I belong, with my friends."

The sorceress's evil eyes looked deep into Kara's, searching. "It seems I still can be surprised."

Adriane glanced at Kara suspiciously. "What does she mean one always turns dark and betrays the others?"

"I guess the wishing crystal went to my head," Kara said in a rush. "All I could think about was replacing the power crystal I lost. But I'm not dark. Are you?"

"No," Adriane answered firmly. "I was trapped by the power crystal but I'm okay now."

"I am so relieved," Kara cried, hugging her friend.

"Me, too." Adriane threw her arms around Kara. Neither of them had turned dark. And Drake was alive!

"Keep your friends, blazing star, it doesn't matter." The Dark Sorceress swept her cloak around her and turned to the portal. "Your time has come and gone. Whereas mine is just beginning. Oh," she swept her hand through the magic snaking from the portal, "don't worry about all this magic, my shadow creatures will take care of it—and the unicorns as well."

Followed by her monstrous creatures, she stepped through the Gates of Avalon. One by one, the nine prisms of light vanished until nothing was left, not even the key.

The mages had been shut out.

Adriane and Kara looked at one another in disbelief.

"Wait," Kara said. "If you didn't turn dark and I didn't, then…"

Emily swayed back and forth over the ferret's body. But she was not healing her friend. Caught in the dark weaving spell, she directed the unicorns along the magic web—the Spider Witch's web.

"Ozzie, get up," Kara ordered.

"Ozzie?" Adriane's voice wavered.

Ozzie's chest was still, his body limp.

Too shocked to speak, Adriane and Kara rushed to the ferret.

He wasn't breathing.

"Emily, do something!" Kara screamed.

Lyra nosed her friend, mewling in pain.

Dreamer howled an anguished cry.

"Please, Ozzie! Don't leave us!" Adriane sobbed.

But the ferret was already gone.

The mages huddled on the stone floor, grief stricken.

But that meant little to the healer now, for the Prophecy of Three had come to pass, just as the sorceress said it would.

One will follow her heart

Adriane had followed her heart. She'd found her home at Ravenswood.

One will change utterly and completely

Kara had changed many times to become the blazing star.

One will see in darkness

Tears streaming down their faces, the warrior and the blazing star gaped at Emily—the one nobody ever worried about, the most constant, the most compassionate, the one always ready to help.

And now, when she needed her friends the most, they had failed her.

"Emily, can't you see us?"

"Emily, we're right here!"

It was too late.

Emily had seen in darkness. She had seen dark magic. And now she had become the dark mage.

BESTIARY & CREATURE GUIDE

KOBOLD

NEUTRAL

$\mathcal{B}$ear-like creatures with coarse black hair, kobolds live in the cold, misty bogs of the Otherworlds. They are territorial and fiercely protective of their race. Kobold Shamans have a rich tradition of using magic to make talismans and amulets to identify individual tribes.

GWYX,
WARRIOR DRAGON
NEUTRAL

*G*wylrrtrwrx (Gwyx) is a young dragon on a warrior quest to save Dragon Home. He is about Drake's size, but has rich black scales and deep purple slashes zigzagged across his leathery wings. Dragons have shunned the worlds of humans, preferring to stay with their own kind. It is forbidden for dragons to bond with humans, so Gwyx is extremely surprised when he meets Adriane and Drake.

SHADOW LEECH

EVIL

$\mathcal{A}$ magic hungry parasite from the most foul regions of the Astral Plains. These deadly creatures possess a mouth full of disgusting fangs that penetrate the skin of a magic user, rendering its victim paralyzed and helpless. A shadow leech will only release its host once the magic is completely drained.

SPIDER WITCH'S
SPIDERS

EVIL

*T*he Spider Witch controls a vast army of giant spiders. These web weaving arachnids serve their mistress by spinning dark magic into whatever pattern she desires. The witch's plan is to unleash thousands of them to re-weave the magic web into a new web only she will control.

RACHEL ROBERTS
ON DARK MAGE

*T*HERE'S AN OLD saying: "The darkest hour is always before the dawn." I believe that to be true. There are times in our lives when we feel alone, face trouble, or feel scared by the darkness the world can sometimes force upon us. It's these times that true courage is tested. We must never give in to despair, even when it feels like the night will never end. You have the magic within to meet any challenge and carry on. A new dawn will always shine its way into your heart.